Jonathan grasped her by the upper arms

"Imagine, talk like that between you and me, Camilla. It's rather ridiculous, isn't it, when once we thought we'd spend the rest of our lives together? When we planned to be one, in flesh and spirit."

Camilla said in a low, intense tone, "Let go of me. I told you in my letter I thought it had all been one huge romantic mistake, that I couldn't marry you. I simply stopped loving you."

She'd had to say that. Because something, she didn't know what, held her back from flinging her knowledge of his dishonesty in his face.

"How strange," he said. "When your grandmother came to England, she said she knew you still carried a torch for me. Camilla, I warn you, I'll proceed with caution."

A Lamp for Jonathan

Essie Summers

Harlequin Books

TORONTO • NEW YORK • LONDON
AMSTERDAM • PARIS • SYDNEY • HAMBURG
STOCKHOLM • ATHENS • TOKYO • MILAN

Original hardcover edition published in 1982
by Mills & Boon Limited

ISBN 0-373-02622-6

Harlequin Romance first edition May 1984

To
SARAH DALEY,
my granddaughter, friend, and
part-time secretary.

CHAPTER ONE

STANDING by the window of the room where her grandmother lay sleeping, Camilla gazed out over the dreamy peace of the Bay of Islands as seen from the sheltered inlet of Reikorangi, the Gate of Heaven.

Elinor Hallows had the same peaceful look. The silver sheen of the twilit waters was repeated in the sweep of the hair brushed back in two wings from that serene forehead . . . but that look would be dispelled in an instant if she opened her eyes, those black, snapping, mischievous eyes.

A faint dread caught at Camilla's heart momentarily. Was that look too peaceful? Was age catching up with her at last? With her indomitable grandmother? Camilla gave herself a mental shake. It had been nothing more than a touch of 'flu, and that was often followed by a loss of energy.

She heard footsteps coming across the bridge of the creek, then changing resonance as they came to the path of old millstones across the orchard lawn. Oh, good, that was Aunt Rose coming from next door. At the same moment the wicket gate on to the lane creaked. She must remember to put a drop of oil on it. High heels this time, she thought. She looked down. Oh, heavens, it was Edie again!

Something like friendship, for want of a better name, existed between Grandmother and Edie. On Elinor's side it was the case of an old habit, lasting from schooldays. On Edie's, the dependence of a light, frivolous nature upon a stronger. Even in old age she simply hadn't the sense she was born with.

Camilla went out of the French windows that led on to the old Colonial verandah and on to the lawn to greet them both. Much better having Edie ask how Gran

7

was out here in a tone that suggested she was at death's door.

She spoke clearly and firmly herself. 'Oh, how nice of you, Edie, to pop in. Gran's so used to seeing umpteen people in the course of her business day, I'm sure she must get bored with all this rest we've insisted on.'

Edie's tone was surprised. 'You mean she's taken a turn for the better? Really? Now I'd have thought——'

Aunt Rose's voice came in, gay, seemingly carefree. 'Oh, she'll be bossing us round in no time again, just to pay us out for having the nerve to insist on her taking it easy. I'm sure she's just humouring us. Come on in.'

But Elinor still had her eyes closed. Maybe she didn't feel like Edie's prattle just now. Oh, well, Aunt Rose would keep the conversation going. Camilla said, 'I'm going out to plant the asters—Gran thinks no garden should be without asters in autumn, and I forgot them.'

'I only hope,' said Edie, 'that she's spared to see them bloom. Such a waste otherwise. Because we could scarcely bear to look at them if not.'

Camilla laughed. 'Gran would be the first to condemn an idea like that, Edie. Over at Kerikeri some of those roses and fruit trees have been growing there since 1828, their vines too. Don't you remember that Gran drinks a toast to the pioneers who planted those vines every Christmas Day? She'll have the hide off me if I don't get these in. When she stops dozing why not get her to play Scrabble?'

Edie was shocked. '*Scrabble?* It's just not ... not right, not seemly. She'll have other things to think about when ... when she's conscious.'

It was too much for Elinor. Her crêpey eyelids flew up, the black eyes snapped. 'Edie, you're a fool. The years don't make you any wiser. Supposing I *had* been dying, don't you know the last sense to go is hearing? Many a thing better left unsaid has been uttered when a person seems in a coma, and words can penetrate even the mists ... and hurt. There was someone in a book once, now who? Some Elizabethan courtier, I fancy. It was said of him that he'd joke in the very mouth of hell ... well, if that's so, surely old Elinor Hallows can play Scrabble at the Gate of Heaven?' She waved her hand towards the view framed by her windows, of the two headlands that guarded the inlet and gave it its name.

Edie looked apologetically at Rose Giddings and said, 'I don't mind. I'm used to her calling me names, but you'd think at *this* stage she'd——'

Rose burst out laughing. 'You don't have to excuse Mother to me, Edie. Come on, I'll put this bed-tray across and get out the Scrabble. She's getting up tomorrow, says she has things to attend to.'

Edie looked horrified. 'You're not going to let her take up the reins again, surely?'

Rose said, 'I've an idea it's not the business she's thinking of. Run along, Camilla, and get your asters in,' and when the tall figure with the dark honey-coloured hair had disappeared she added drily, 'It's my opinion my dear mama is up to mischief. She has that cut about her jib.'

Camilla hadn't gone far. She wanted the asters to grow in thick clumps along the path that edged the verandah bed, where clematis and wistaria twined around the posts. She was hidden from the windows by a screen of tangled twigs and leaves as she knelt and trowelled and slopped water into the holes she dug. What had Aunt Rose meant? She raised her head now and listened with all her might.

Aunt Rose said, 'And don't assume that angelic expression, Mother. I'm sure there's something, and what's more that Edward knows about it. He'd abet you in anything.'

She heard her grandmother chuckle, 'There are no flies on Edward. There's a son-in-law after my own heart. He'd never think I would shuffle off this mortal coil before I've seen completed all I want to see. I've never liked unfinished business.'

Edie said curiously, 'What do you mean, Elinor? I've a feeling you don't mean some big new deal in antiques.'

Elinor retorted, 'You're dead right. Once in a while, Edie, you show a bit of gumption. This bout of 'flu has been a little setback, nothing more. I wouldn't let it lay me low for long. That'd be an entire waste of that trip I took to Britain. I can still pull a few strings. I'm not in my dotage yet, believe me.'

A crease appeared in the centre of Camilla's brows. What on earth was Gran up to now? She heard Aunt Rose drop the Scrabble pieces, sound rueful, start gathering them up. Had she done that for a diversion? Did she suspect something and didn't want Edie to know? And why should Camilla suddenly feel uneasy? Gran had been very headstrong over that trip, had flatly refused to take anyone with her, not even Aunt Rose who could have been spared quite easily.

She'd done a little buying, naturally, but not as much as on her former trips. Also she'd come back with a very smug expression, so noticeable that Uncle Edward said he expected to hear she'd found some long wished-for treasure for her own home, or managed to secure one for a valued client. But no. She had merely said the English countryside was as lovely as ever, London just as fascinating though even more crowded, and how wonderful it was to find people so unchanged.

She had made no secret of the fact that she had stayed with Kathleen and Sylvester Lemaire, but despite the fact that Jonathan Lemaire worked in his grandparents' business still, she hadn't as much as mentioned him. Perhaps he no longer lived with them.

Gran had never uttered his name from the time Camilla had broken her engagement to him, sending his ring back to him in London. So for sure Camilla wouldn't ask after him. Gran talked of Randall and Stephen, Jonathan's elder brothers, and of their families, but not of Jonathan, nor of Prue, his sister, which was also strange.

If only she'd mentioned him in passing, then Camilla could have been equally casual in response. It would have given her the details that despite her own self-control, she longed to hear, hungered to hear ... what he had done with his life, if he had married.

At the thought her teeth came down on her lower lip. Stop thinking those things, she told herself. It only hurts. It was so stupid to still have this yearning. He didn't deserve one atom of her thoughts. She'd lived five years without him. So she would live out the rest of her life, undisturbed by regret, nostalgia, that unaccountable sense of irreparable damage and loss.

If only she could get really interested in someone else! She'd tried, only to find it wouldn't work. It was maddening. She'd start off by telling herself she *was* interested, only to find in a couple of weeks or so that she was utterly bored. And in honesty, because it wasn't fair to waste anyone's time, or raise hopes, she'd let it peter out. Occasionally she and Greg Peterson would partner each other to some function, but that was pure friendship, and suited them both.

Camilla pulled herself up with a jerk. One man didn't have to matter so much, for so long. It had been her own fault, imagining he was her ideal man. Well, he'd had feet of clay. Lots of people got disillusioned. There were more things in life than romance and marriage. She couldn't have had a more satisfying career, buying and selling antiques, meeting tourists from all over the world, come to see the Colonial charm of Hallows Green, that exquisite blend of the old and the new ... English old-world beauty transported to this far-flung corner of what had once been Queen Victoria's Empire. Not only transported, but harmonised into this South Pacific paradise so that two forms of beauty had become an even greater one.

Even the shadow of losing both parents when she was small had been less tragic than it might have been, because she had had Grandmother and in those days Grandfather too, and Aunt Rose and Uncle Edward. Cousin Rob had been as a brother, and he was still so close at hand, running his father's launch service as it had always been run. The ties of family life and ancestry were very strong in Reikorangi.

Aunt Rose called out, 'If you're finished, Camilla, you might make us some coffee before Edie has to go. I brought some cheese straws over and some cherry cakes.'

Camilla grinned to herself. Aunt Rose could well have done it herself, but obviously didn't want to leave the dilly Edie with her mother. She smoothed the soil, stripped off her gloves, said, 'It's as good as done. I'm dying for some!'

As she went by the door she heard her grandmother say, 'I've been over the 'flu some time, Edie, but whenever I'm expecting to be busier than usual, I rest beforehand.'

Busier? But this was just late September and the tourist trade didn't get underway till Labour Weekend at the end of October. Surely Gran wasn't going to have one of her old-fashioned spring-cleaning bouts? Having got her through September they'd hoped she might overlook it this year.

She hoped Gran wouldn't overdo things when she was away at Russell across the Bay tomorrow. She simply had to see the legatees of the Old Dyswood House to find out if they were going to let Hallows Antiques have the things they'd decided against keeping. They had had a valuer up from Auckland: Camilla had insisted on that. Much as she coveted the stuff, Hallows House had the reputation of absolute integrity to maintain. It sometimes cut profits, but their standing was high. David Hallows, Camilla's grandfather, had been known for half a century for the ultimate in honesty.

This was why it was a good thing she'd seen the writing on the wall as far as Jonathan Lemaire was concerned. If ever she brought a husband into the business, he must have the same standards as David Hallows. Standard that even went back to old Joshua Hallows, the first trader of pioneer days at Reikorangi.

The next morning was glorious and Grandmother was up at her usual time with no hint of the languor that had characterised her the last week. She flicked a feather duster here and there, brought in some violets, purple and white, for the vase in the spare room, then began tidying the huge linen closets in the upstairs hall.

Camilla said uncertainly, 'Gran, you won't overdo it, will you? I know what you're like. You've regained some energy, and you're likely to expend it all in one day if you aren't wise. I wish I wasn't going out on this first day up for you. But I'll be home for a late lunch, say one o'clock. I'm going by Opua, the car ferry's so frequent.'

'Don't fuss, child. And don't hurry, either. The Dyswoods' stuff is important. Get that ferry, or the one after. Don't attempt an earlier one just because you're fidgeting about me. It's a glorious day. Now be off and don't fuss. I'll just potter. Rose will show any tourists that come round the historic wing.'

Camilla kissed her and was off, driving her late model Japanese car towards and beyond Paihia. She had a most satisfactory morning. The stuff she'd purchased would be picked up another time, carefully packed by Edward and Rose, and brought across in one of his launches, but beside her, on the front seat, carefully wedged into a box with lashings of tissue, was something that would delight Grandmother's heart . . . the pair of china candlesticks that her own grandmother had given one of the Dyswoods' forebears as a wedding present. Elinor would be delighted. She would have no idea that in the gift Camilla knew a secret delight of her own. Long ago she and Jonathan had visited the old lady Dyswood, and she had told them the story of the candle-

sticks. She had said, 'When you marry Jonathan, I'll
give them to you for your wedding present.'

It had been said so simply and naturally, because then
Camilla had been wearing Jonathan's heavy old antique
ring, set with a single ruby, on her finger. How she
missed the feel of that ring! Which was quite stupid.
Material things didn't matter against the true loss ...
that sense of having something torn out of one's heart
and life.

But now those candlesticks, lovely in their crafts-
manship and dear in their own association for generations, would sit on the mantelpiece at Hallows House
and Camilla would look at them and remember. And
nobody would ever know what they meant to her.
Because naturally, Jonathan would never come again to
the inlet called the Gate of Heaven.

Camilla left the houses of Russell behind and drove
the Corona down towards Okiato Point. She smiled to
herself, because *kiato* meant 'a receptacle for holding
sacred objects'.

She patted the wheel of the Corona. 'That's what you
are today,' she informed her modern vehicle, 'because
these candlesticks mean so much to me and they meant
so much to my forebears of long ago.' She turned a
corner and came within sight of the sparkling waters
again, then slackened pace because the car-ferry wasn't
even on its way but was still loading vehicles on at
Opua.

A big beach-ball bounced across the road and she
slackened pace still more. A child might easily hurtle
across in pursuit. She turned her golden-brown head to
the right. Ah yes, there was a father and his children, a
boy and a girl, not more than four years old, either of
them, if that. She pulled to a stop.

The man, still some distance away, nodded his thanks,
took a hand of each, and crossed the road to the further
verge with them, then let them go to dive into the long
grass and bushes to search for it.

Then he turned, came across towards the car on the passenger side as if he wanted to ask something. As he neared it he smiled.

Camilla had an instant dizzying sensation as if the world had turned upside down. It couldn't be. It just couldn't be. But it was.

He leaned bronzed forearms upon the open window ledge, said, 'Hullo, Camilla. Your grandmother said I'd find you at the car-ferry, on either this one, or on the one before. The children just couldn't wait to see you.'

She knew her colour had ebbed and hated the knowledge that he couldn't help but notice it. Often, naturally enough, she'd wondered if they would ever meet again. Not in New Zealand, she'd thought, but possibly in London, if she ever made it to Sotheby's or Christie's. She would be cool, elegant, poised, uncaring—a top career woman.

Instead of that he'd given her a shock and knew it. He'd enjoyed this, the beast. It was written all over him in the audacious glint in his eye, the supreme confidence of him. He was laughing inwardly. She had to do something. She put a hand on her door and got out. That gave her a moment in which to recover. She let her bag drop out and knew that stooping to recover it would bring the blood back to her cheeks. She tossed it on to her seat, came round the front of the car and said, 'Why, Jonathan, where on earth did you spring from?'

Before he could answer her, he turned quickly to look at the children, said, 'Victoria, Perry . . . don't cross the road again. This is——'

He got no further. Camilla could have bitten her tongue out the next moment. She was absolutely astounded to hear her own voice say: 'Perry! *Peregrine!* How *could* you? You knew I wanted——' she stopped, appalled.

She thought he grinned sardonically. 'Yes, of course I knew you wanted a son called Peregrine. But that was when you were going to marry *me*. And perhaps you could remember it was a family name of mine . . . not yours. *My* grandmother's maiden name. We wanted it for *our* son. You didn't have a monopoly on the name. Tell me, if you'd married someone else, would you really have had the nerve to call your son Peregrine?'

She managed to say coldly, 'Of course not. The question doesn't arise, anyway. It—it was just somehow surprising, that's all. I wouldn't have said anything had I known. Gran never told me you'd married. She must have known after this trip.'

Her mind was racing. By the age of these children, he'd married very soon after she'd broken their engagement. One of these sudden decisions on the rebound, she supposed. Well, who cared?

At that moment the small boy, retrieving the ball one second ahead of his sister, yelled, 'Vicky, look out! You'll trip!' then looking up towards the car, 'She's losing her knickers again, Uncle Jonathan!'

Again Camilla was surprised to hear her voice say: '*Uncle* Jonathan! Really, why didn't you say?'

He grinned evilly. 'It was interesting to see you leap to conclusions, the same as ever . . . and I enjoyed your reaction. Let me rescue my niece. Those knickers are a plaguey nuisance. Her mother might have warned me, or put another pair on her,' and he leapt down the bank, laughing. *Laughing*. Camilla felt crosser than ever at knowing such a flood of relief pour over her. She ought to feel like boiling him in oil. She told herself she *was* furious really. It was only reaction to being made a fool of, for such a giveaway. Well, now she was in command of herself she'd soon show him how indifferent she was!

He was back in a moment, bearing Victoria in his arms because she was too hampered to walk. 'Peregrine, this is Camilla. Camilla, this is Victoria. Their surname is Lane. My sister Prue's pair.'

Peregrine said promptly, 'Do you think we could call you Aunt Camilla? We're a bit short on aunts since we came to New Zealand.'

How set a child back? But it linked her with Jonathan. She forced herself to say cordially, 'Yes, of course, Perry. How long have you been in New Zealand?'

'Six months. We live in Auckland, only Mummy suddenly had a chance to go to Raratonga for a week with Dad and she was stumped, but Uncle Jonathan arrived in the nick of time and said it was easy, he'd just take us up here with him.'

Camilla swallowed. 'Did he indeed? What a very happy solution.'

'Yuh. There are lots of boats, aren't there? And millions of islands.'

'Well, about a hundred and fifty islands,' admitted Camilla . . . then she twinkled and added, 'That's over a gross . . . and a gross sounds almost as good as a million, don't you think?'

'Good,' said Jonathan. 'It's still got a sense of humour . . . so perhaps you'd be able to deal with the little matter of my niece's knickers before the car-ferry gets here, eh?'

She had a feeling this couldn't be true. She took a scrap of sprigged cotton from Jonathan, examined the top and said with relief, 'Thank goodness these are the kind with proper elastic, not just shirring. It's just perished. I'll only need to tie a knot in it if I can hook it out. I know . . . the first aid kit has got a pair of tweezers in for splinters. That'll get it.'

Jonathan heaved an exaggerated sigh of relief as she pulled them up on his squirming niece. 'You can see just how badly I needed you at this moment.'

Their eyes locked. Camilla looked away, said, 'The car-ferry's almost in . . . how did you get here?'

'By car—mine. But there was no point in bringing it across . . . we left it at the other side. It filled in time coming over, when you didn't drive off the earlier one. Hop in the back, kids, I'll get in front.'

'Be very careful,' warned Camilla. 'And take that box on your knee. It's not for the shop, it's for

Grandmother. Something she's wanted for a long, long time.' Might as well tell him—for Gran would be bound to show him, unknowing he'd seen them before.

'Good show. I'll look after it.'

As they drove down, the children madly chattering behind them, she said in a low tone, 'Here for a holiday with Prue, are you? For how long?'

'Now why does that sound, for some reason, inhospitable? It really isn't polite to ask guests when they're going to shove off, the moment they arrive.'

She tightened her lips. 'You're hardly *my* guest. Gran didn't even see fit to tell me you were coming. So the rules of etiquette don't apply.'

Jonathan said, 'I didn't believe her when she said it to me in London, but it's true. That you've grown rather hard.'

'I don't think I really want to know what you and Gran said about me. It doesn't matter to me.'

'No?' His tone held disbelief.

Camilla said, 'You haven't told me how long you're staying. I'd like to know how long in New Zealand? How long in Bay of Islands?'

'Same answer for both. Very simple. For the rest of my life!'

She felt the blood drumming in her ears. Shock upon shock.

'Don't be ridiculous! Why should you?'

'Because my livelihood will be here.'

She swallowed. 'How? Why?'

She just couldn't believe it when he answered in a level, matter-of-fact tone, 'Because your grandmother is letting me have one-third of the business. Retaining one-third for herself, and of course the other third is yours already.'

Camilla couldn't speak. The implications were too many, too complicated. She opened her mouth once or twice, but no sound came out. It was too hideous. What on earth had gone on in London?

Unforgivably Jonathan laughed. She said between her teeth, 'I'll be manoeuvring this car aboard in a moment. We'll discuss it later—alone. Not with even my grandmother present.'

He added, 'Get your blood sugar down, Camilla Hallows. I didn't allow her to do it. Not as a gift, I mean. I've *bought* the third—a neat arrangement. The bulk of the purchase is coming out in antiques by shipment already on the ocean. My grandparents and your grandmother are very happy about it.'

'How nice for them. I suppose my feelings don't count.'

'Your grandmother was sure that in the long run it would be in your best interests.'

When she could speak again, her voice was cool, distant: 'It makes one realise that even one's nearest and dearest ... to wit my grandmother ... can be utterly mistaken. It's as if she never really knew me.'

'Here we are,' he said. 'This has been a shock to you. Would you like me to take the car on board?'

Her recoil was instant. 'You've got to be joking! I need no help from you in anything at all, Jonathan Lemaire. Now or ever.' She called over her shoulder, 'Just look, children ... that man's got a monkey on his shoulder. How wonderful for you! I know him. He'll let you stroke him.' She ran smoothly on to the barge, got out and said, 'Gino, may these children pat Beppo?'

The pilot of the vessel suddenly looked more closely at Jonathan and said, 'I knew you years ago, didn't I? I'd a feeling that your face was familiar when I took you over.' He looked from Jonathan to Camilla, and knowledge dawned, also a faint embarrassment. Camilla realised that look was something she'd have to get used to in the next few weeks. It said, as plainly as could be: *Good heavens! these two used to be engaged ... now I wonder...?* How could Gran have done this to her?

Jonathan was quite unmoved. He said, looking about him at the still waters they were to cross, the bright new houses, opulent-looking, that nestled into the heights above the bay, the luxuriant emerald growth of the trees, the flamboyant splashes of colour in the semi-tropical creepers that rioted over patios and terraces, 'I'd forgotten how beautiful it was . . . no wonder I just had to come back.'

The pilot grinned. 'Couldn't live anywhere else myself . . . though I daresay people all over the world say that very thing about their own place.'

'True. But this has a magic all its own.'

Camilla felt as if she moved in a dream. This couldn't really be happening. The children were engrossed with the charms of the captivating monkey.

She said in a low voice to Jonathan, 'You had no thoughts that it might be too much for my grandmother, having two young children?'

'With *you* there? I hadn't thought of Hallie running round after them. I thought of you. You were marvellous with Rob's children. And Hallie assured me that in that, at least, you hadn't changed.'

He sounded anything but apologetic for landing three extra people upon the household. She said so, adding, 'A woman wouldn't think of doing it. Men just don't realise.'

'Oh, I don't know. After all, Uncle Edward was the first one I contacted when Prue got this chance. Aunt Rose was across at Hallow Green. He was so keen that he thought he had all the say-so. I had insisted he put it to Aunt Rose and Hallie on the quiet and that I'd ring back to make sure it was all right.'

'Uncle Edward, as you know, is simply daft on children. He's got a heart of butter.' She looked at Jonathan as they cast off, as coldly as she could. 'You didn't dare ask *me*. You knew I'd have refused.' Her lip curled.

'Of course. Hallie said in England that we must present you with a *fait accompli*, that you'd be quite unable to upset the apple-cart then and would just have to lump it.' His eyes raked her face. 'It's hard to credit, yet——'

'What's hard to credit?'

'That brown eyes can look so cold. I used to be quite batty about your eyes in my green and salad days, didn't I? Remember that poem I wrote about them? . . . "your eyes like woodland pools, so brown and tender . . ." I've always thought that blue eyes or grey eyes can look cold very easily, but never brown eyes . . . your eyes. How wrong one can be!'

She said, still coldly, 'I find this conversation idiotic. You make everything too personal. I'm a totally different person from the idealistic, even gullible girl I used to be. I'll put up with you coming into the firm, seeing I can't do anything about it, and I'll not let it colour my attitude to these children—that wouldn't be fair—but don't try me too far, Jonathan Lemaire. For Gran's sake, even if she *is* a wicked old lady, I'd like Hallow Green to stay a harmonious sort of place. But watch your step.'

The car-ferry slid up on to the sloping shore, and the cars came off. Camilla asked, 'Which is your car? You're in a hired one, I suppose?'

'No, hired cars are for tourists, I'm staying. That's mine there, the Jag. I've been in New Zealand a month— I got it in Auckland. Right, kids, come along.'

Victoria turned, held Camilla's hand, 'I want to go with *her*.' Peregrine said simply, 'Me too. I've never ridden in a Toyota Corona before.'

'Down with Jags,' said Jonathan, grinning.

'You'd better follow,' said Camilla. 'I'm no speed-fiend.'

Peregrine opened wide dark eyes so like Jonathan's it was uncanny and said, 'Neither's Uncle Jonathan. Dad goes much faster.'

'Children are so fair,' commended his uncle. '*They* never hit below the belt. I'll follow. And you needn't worry about lunch. The children have been promised fish and chips on the beach at Paihia. Not in a res-taurant, out of the paper. And green fizz. We'll all have fish and chips and green fizz. I told Hallie and Aunt Rose.'

'And that, of course, would be all right with them,' Camilla said wearily.

The children's chatter stopped her doing what she'd hoped to do, driving alone, which was think it out, decide how she was going to treat all this, what she would say to Gran and Aunt Rose and Uncle Edward . . . to Rob and Sarah and Caroline. How she would be watched this next little while, when people all about Reikorangi would realise her one-time fiancé had come back and was a partner in the firm to boot.

Peregrine filled her in with lots of family details. Dad was in the travel business and was with the Auckland branch for three or four years. But there was a chance they might stay. Mum just loved New Zealand and they lived in a lovely bay . . . Kohimarama . . . on Auckland harbour, and now Uncle Jonathan had come out here to live, she didn't feel so cut off from her family. He was four, he informed her, nearly five, and would start school in February, but Victoria was only three and a half, whereupon Victoria chipped in, 'But I can do up zips better'n you, Perry. I mean the kind what comes apart, he can never get them together in the right place.'

'But I can tie knots better, and she doesn't know her left foot from her right.'

Camilla chuckled. 'I still couldn't, when I started school. I was such a duffer at that, and telling the time. It always seemed daft to me that when both pointers were on seven, they called it twenty-five to seven. It just didn't make sense to me.'

'That was the trouble with being born in the olden days,' said Perry solemnly, 'before digital clocks were even invented. *I* think they ought to have all clocks digital now.'

They swung round the last bend in the road and the glorious spread of the Bay of Islands shimmered in front of them, dotted with countless islands, emerald against the blue. Paihia lay below, rimming its bay, and spreading up into its own green valley. Launches were making out towards the heads for deep-sea game fishing, speedboats in coral and blue were skimming the waters, the sands lay golden and curving. Beyond on the same side were the grounds of the Treaty House at Waitangi, where New Zealand became part of Victoria's Empire on February 6th, 1840. Then the sparkling waters had been black with canoes, and the sound of matchless Maori voices, singing, had drowned out the bird-song.

If anyone had told Camilla that morning as she ate breakfast that her next meal would be fish and chips eaten on the Paihia beach, with Jonathan and two children, she'd have thought them crazy.

Jonathan was so outrageously casual about it, as if it was nothing to be wondered at at all. As if she had nothing better to do than wander on the sands with his niece and nephew, picking up shells, and splashing barefooted in the water. He was wearing tussore-coloured lightweight slacks, a corn-coloured woven top with brown edges to the collar and a brown and white polka-dotted cravat loosely knotted at his bronzed throat. He tanned easily, of course, and in the month he'd been in New Zealand, it would be easy to get up a tan on the Kohimarama Beach.

The children were happily trailing long strands of seaweed behind them. He caught Camilla studying him, said, 'Like what you see, madam?'

Her brows twitched together. 'You've changed greatly, Jonathan. You were never vain before.'

He chuckled. 'Would you have wanted me to stay the way I was five years ago? I was never an admirer of Peter Pan. I like people to grow up. I didn't think you were studying my looks, idiot. I thought you were looking for clues as to the sort of man I'd become. Right?'

She gave him what was meant to be a levelling look. 'I'm not really interested in the sort of man you've become, Jonathan. You're here, apparently to stay, and as I can't do anything about that, I'll go along with it, in a business sort of way. We don't meet on the same ground as we did before. We've both changed. Times have changed. Our world has changed.'

He said slowly, 'The only change that could matter would be if someone else has taken the place I once held in your life. But no one has ... that's true, isn't it, Camilla? Or so your grandmother told me when she came to London.'

Camilla brushed back a strand of hair that had blown across her forehead as if she brushed aside an un-welcome idea. 'Let's get something straight, Jonathan. There isn't anyone in particular, at the moment. But I think you'd better understand something. I've changed radically. I was a romantic goose five years ago, and not discriminating at that. I've found now what I really want in life. Not every girl desires marriage. I've got a career, I love my work. Hallows Green is the be-all and end-all of my existence, and trading in antiques. My roots are here, back to the early days, when my an-cestors first planted their corn and their vines, first felled the trees for the timbers of their house. It's become one of the historical showplaces of New Zealand. Not under a Trust, but still ours, still lived in by the family, pre-served and loved. It satisfies me.'

'Does it? Wouldn't it be more satisfying still if you knew someone who would love it as much, who would have the same ties of blood, would follow on with your work into the twenty-first century? Your son? The little Peregrine you dreamed of? The small Elinor, named for your grandmother, that we planned once?'

She said abruptly, 'Aunt Rose's children have the same blood in them. Her Caroline is unbelievably knowledgeable about antiques, and even her small Sarah can recognise some fakes. And Cousin Rob has two children already. Hallows Green will never pass out of the family.'

'Caroline and Sarah, as they grow up, will probably

be the sort of wives who follow their men. Men who may take them away from Bay of Islands. Think on that.'

Camilla traced a clover-leaf pattern in the sand with the toe of her sandal. 'I don't have to do any thinking. My life is staying the same. This three-pronged partnership, Jonathan, will have to be just a business association. I'll lump it, not like it. You have the children here for a week. Right . . . we'll give them a good time. They must be at Hallows Green, but after that, no doubt, you'll hunt round for a flat. You'll want a life of your own. You'll find Reikorangi quite changed. Motels and ownership units have sprung up all over the place. The sooner you have a place of your own the better. You ought to start looking for one without delay.'

'Like hell I will,' he said. 'You haven't the ordering of this, you know. You may have grown up at Hallows Green, but it isn't yours. It's your grandmother's home. And she's offered me the room I had when I spent my first holiday here as a kid of twelve. You were seven. And I came back at twenty-five and—and fell in love with you. I wouldn't dream of turning Hallie's offer down. So I'm afraid you're stuck with me, Camilla Hallows.'

She said in a sound just above a whisper, 'I hate you, Jonathan Lemaire. I just hate you for doing this to me. You've destroyed the peace and harmony of my ordered existence.'

There was a derisive note in his answering voice that rasped her nerves. 'Sounds tame to me. And this is the girl who, at seven, declared passionately that she'd rather have horrid things happen to her than nothing happening at all. That was when I accidentally walloped you with my tennis racquet and knocked you out, remember. It was rather sweet of you. You did it to save me getting blamed, I know. Nobody can change that much, Camilla.'

She wouldn't answer him.

CHAPTER TWO

UNREALITY still gripped Camilla as she drove inland from Paihia, past the beauty of the Haruru Falls, with always in her driving mirror the image of Jonathan's car coming steadily behind hers. They drove past the turn-off to Kerikeri, that historical inlet so similar to their own more distant bay, through cuttings and forested areas, till they turned right and began running down to the Reikorangi Village, between the luxuriant sheltered orchards of kiwi fruit, tamarillos, grapefruit and oranges, tangelos and mandarines.

Everywhere was evidence of early Colonial buildings and houses beautifully preserved, gleaming through the foliage of clustering trees in splendour of white paint on the wooden walls, red and green roofs with here and there the mellow greyness of wooden shingles. Beyond, at every winding of the road, glittered the faceted waters of the inlet with the early afternoon sun on it, and farther out, the green-clad sheltering arms of the Gate of Heaven. A small world, loved by Camilla with a passion almost frightening in its intensity. Yet it was one she'd been prepared to leave five years ago, if Jonathan had desired to return to his own place, London. But now this was her whole life, a place of serenity, where she bought and sold those things that were woven into the fabric of Colonial history, to kindred people who also loved those things. Only with Jonathan's return, serenity had fled.

Suddenly Jonathan caught up and passed her, then curved into a long wide green verge ahead and signalled for her to stop. She pulled in behind him. He came back to her, said, 'Camilla, I want to speak to you. Children, stay for a moment or two.'

He opened the car and she got out, walked to the rear

26

of the car with him and stood facing him, tall, cool, yet hostile-eyed.

He said abruptly, 'It's about Hallie. I don't want her upset.'

Camilla felt the warmth of anger rise in her, but with an effort kept it from showing in her cheeks. She said, 'I hardly need you to tell me how to treat Hallie. She's *my* grandmother, not yours, remember. The dearest person left to me on earth. Maybe if someone else was trying to pull strings as if we were puppets, I'd call her an interfering old lady, but it's my grandmother who's doing it. She's doing it out of love for me, even if she's vastly mistaken. She's got no idea why——'

His eyes were keen. 'Go on. She's no idea why you ... why you what?'

She waved a hand dismissingly. 'Let that go. It doesn't matter.'

'It does matter. I want to know why you stopped. Why you're afraid to finish that sentence.'

'Then, as Gran used to say when I was little and wanted something I couldn't have, want must be your master. It was something I thought better of saying. I'm not quite the impulsive girl I used to be, Jonathan Lemaire. I've learned discretion.'

'Possibly. You've learned a *little* control. But some feelings still show. This, for instance ... at one time you'd have coloured right up with anger and let fly at me, not caring what you said, but you're not as cool as you're trying to be. It shows here,' and he reached out and ran his fingers across the hollow of her throat. 'You've a red patch right here.'

She jerked back from his touch and said hastily, 'You told me back there, when I said you'd taken a risk bringing the children up here as if you were certain of your welcome, that you were sure I hadn't changed so much that I'd make children feel unwelcome. What then makes you feel I'd hurt my grandmother over this?'

'I was fairly sure you wouldn't, but for her sake I had to make sure. And, to make our arrival easier, I thought I'd ask you just how you're going to appear, what line you're going to take.'

She said crisply, 'Then it will be interesting for you to find out, won't it? In about another ten minutes. I'm not working in with you on this, Jonathan. You knew, you must have known, when you and Grandmother hatched this devilish plan, that there were bound to be repercussions. I'm deeply hurt that this ... a business arrangement, should have been taken without consulting me. But I'll put it down to the vagaries of old age, and not take it out on her.'

Jonathan's lips were pursed. His eyes seemed fixed on some distance above her head. He was considering something. Then, 'It wasn't solely a business arrangement.'

Camilla managed a shrug. 'I won't even try to guess at what you mean. And we should move on. I rather think that the poor old darling, cunning and all as she is, and far too fond of her own way, may just be wondering if she's gone too far this time.'

She went back to her car. So they came to Hallows Green with Jonathan in the lead.

As her grandmother turned from the little rosewood desk where she was doing household accounts, and looked at them with a little less than her customary head-of-the-household confidence, Camilla crossed to her, wagged a forefinger and said, 'Good afternoon, Madame Machiavelli ... you've been a very naughty girl, but I'll forgive you this time, for the sake of all those wonderful treasures that are on the water. That S-shaped confidante sofa Jonathan mentioned is the very thing Mrs Arkeld from Christchurch wants for the old homestead she's restoring. I'll forgive you anything for the chance to supply that. We'll get a great deal of publicity out of it. Gran, to come down to the prosaic, we've had fish and chips on the beach at Paihia for the sake of the children, but we'd love a cup of tea right now.'

She saw her grandmother look down quickly, and knew she was struggling with emotions, not the least of them relief. She must have had long weeks of anxiety, wondering how her granddaughter would take this interference with her life, ever since flying home from London.

But when she spoke her voice was crisp and controlled. 'Rose has left some fresh scones in the kitchen, and some ginger gems. She remembered those were Jonathan's favourites from boyhood.'

Camilla gave a small chuckle and said carelessly, 'Not to say his tastes have stayed the same, of course. He might have more sophisticated taste-buds now. I know by my own mature preferences.'

They would get the message, these conspirators. That she was changed and it wasn't likely she'd ever slip back into the attachments of yesteryear.

As the day progressed it became evident that the whole family was curious to know how Camilla had taken it. Even Uncle Edward, who had such a heaven-sent facility for letting people live their own lives, came over in the wake of Aunt Rose and the cousins.

Nevertheless, he reacted differently. *They* looked at Camilla and Jonathan apprehensively, then joined with great relief in small talk, but Uncle Edward manoeuvred Camilla into the Small Parlour and came immediately and calmly to the point.

'I didn't know about this, love, till last night, too late to do a thing about it. I dared not act precipitately. Rose had an idea I was worried about something before she went across to Hallie's, and even asked me if her mother had discussed anything with me when I'd been across just before, when you went to pick up your aster plants. I was tempted to warn you, but I thought it might make you take off, perhaps to Australia again, like you did that time years ago when Jonathan flew out to try to make you change your mind. No point in doing that, of course, because this time he's here to stay. So I thought if you got the initial meeting over suddenly, no traumatic hours beforehand anticipating it, it would be best. Well, that hurdle's taken and you've bobbed up like a cork. Good for you!'

'Oh, Uncle Edward, I do love you, even when you're mixing your metaphors,' smiled Camilla. 'But not to worry. All that emotional guff is a thing of the past. This is purely a matter of business. But no deals must go through without my approval. No Maori artifacts we handle are to go overseas—no law-breaking. Hallows must always stand for integrity, making a fair profit, but not ever selling to the collectors I despise who only want things for their rarity, not their beauty.'

Uncle Edward's blue eyes widened, his grizzled brows lifted. 'Why, lass, Jonathan's coming couldn't affect the integrity of the family business. Lemaire's are known for their scrupulous dealings. The only thing that worried me was that you might feel pressured by Hallie into reversing your decision of years ago. However much I'd like it, I believe in the young making their own matches, even their own mistakes. Well, I've had my say. Don't let any of it get under your skin. He'll be a good business associate.'

Camilla felt as she followed him back to the others: *But then you don't know what I know, darling Uncle Edward.*

It was certainly just as well it was a reasonably quiet day in the antique rooms. Of course the tourist rush hadn't really started yet. Because when it did, it rarely let up. Although this was such a remote tip of New Zealand, the superb scenery and the climate and big-game fishing brought people from all over the country and from the four corners of the earth, and the genuine antique lovers and collectors among them often couldn't resist some of the Hallows House treasures, even though shipping costs scarcely made them bargains.

Wilma Manning was their saleswoman, expert at her job, dependable and pleasant.

Camilla, determined to be as formal and punctilious as possible in the circumstances, took Jonathan through to her. Wilma hadn't come to live at Reikorangi till long after Camilla had broken her engagement to Jonathan, so that made it much easier.

Camilla said, 'Wilma, this is Jonathan Lemaire from London—his grandfather runs a business similar to ours—you've probably heard of it. He spent some time in New Zealand as a young man, and his sister lives in Auckland now. He's brought his niece and nephew up here while their parents are in Rarotonga. But he's coming into the business. His grandmother is a life-long friend of Hallie's and she's thought for some time she'd like a man in the business again. She fixed it up when she was in London in June. But nothing's been said till now, when we were sure the business deal had gone through.' Her gaze flickered to Jonathan's and away.

She managed to infuse a little warmth into her tone, 'The exciting thing is that part of the buying-in price is in goods. They're already on the water—real treasures. There's a corner cupboard, curved, that will suit old Hammond Ford, I should think, and some Georgian silverware, among other things, but the crowning glory will be that we've managed to get a *tête-à-tête* sofa at last for that homestead in Canterbury. I'm going to give them a ring tonight.' They chatted on, Wilma full of interest, then Camilla said, 'Mr Lemaire knows the Bay quite well. His grandmother brought him out when he was very young, and then he had another, longer stay in his twenties.'

He couldn't fault her attitude to the children, she knew, though she was aware he watched her closely. Against her will she admired this. Children suffered a great deal from grown-ups taking it out on them when their own lives went awry. Jonathan seemed to be extremely fond of them . . . perhaps he saw in Peregrine the son, name and all, he hadn't been blessed with. For one foolish moment Camilla knew a weakening softness towards him, a wild regret for the unfulfilled promise of five years ago.

Grandmother had surely had a busy and enjoyable time this morning preparing the children's room for them. It had always been sacred to holidaying children, with two little beds, a cot, a dolls' house and a model railway, Beatrix Potter pictures on the walls, loads of books, old and new, on the shelves, and Gran had evidently gone down to the local bookshop and invested in posters of Paddington Bear and Basil Brush to pin on the walls.

The children were somewhat grubby by the time they'd explored their new surroundings, gone hunting for new kittens in the old loft, and crossed the stream on the stepping-stones, and their uncle peeled off their things in the bathroom and dumped them in the same bath, along with plastic ducks and a fleet of boats. Jonathan insisted Camilla helped him.

At last they were into night attire and tucked in. She went to leave the room, but was called back. 'Prue and Wally have a very strong sense of family unity. They hear prayers together whenever they can manage it. We'll continue that.'

He knew she wouldn't refuse in front of the children. She could have shot him. Shared moments like these were dangerous.

But resentment of that didn't last under the age-old spell of children praying. Peregrine's came first and were quite well expressed, with no selfish petitioning. But he finished up, 'And if it could be arranged, God, we'd like a fine day tomorrow to go out with Uncle Edward in his boat, but it's okay by me if the country needs rain.' His eyes shot open, he fixed them on Camilla and said, 'Dad's explained to me that New Zealand's dependent on primary products, mostly, so you've got to be careful how you pray.' He closed his eyes again. 'God bless

Mummy and Daddy and all the folk here and in London, especially the great-grans, Amen.'

Small Victoria took over. She was adorable, and as like her great-grandmother, Hallie's friend, as a three-year-old could be, with streaky gold hair, and great brown eyes in apple-blossom cheeks. She finished up, 'An' God bless Pink Teddy an' Paddington Bear and his marmalade, and Basil Brush and the TV man, and God bless my new bed, and Uncle Jonno and Aunt C'milla, and the new granny, and God bless my curtains, and the mat on the floor, and my dolls' house, and God bless my plate with the bunnies on it . . . an' . . .'

Peregrine shot bolt upright, said, 'You'll have to stop her . . . it goes on for ever . . . she thinks if she keeps it up long enough, it'll postpone the time when you put the light out. She's as cunning as a box of monkeys.'

Victoria kept her eyes buttoned up tightly, said, 'That reminds me, God, bless the monkey on the boat today, and the man who made his little coat an' . . .'

Jonathan bent down, kissed her firmly, said in a tone of great finality, 'And now, goodnight, sweetheart. Sleep tight. It'll be another long, lovely day tomorrow. Night-night, Perry,' and he whisked Camilla out of the room, and into his next door.

They looked at each other and chuckled, silently. There was still enough afterglow to see each other dimly. 'Much better,' whispered Jonathan. 'I pride myself it was a good idea bringing the children with me. You're almost human.'

Camilla freed her elbow from his grip. It was hard to quarrel in a whisper, but those children must get settled. It came out like a hiss. 'Don't trade on that. Whatever I do for Gran's sake and the children's doesn't mean a thing. We may have to share moments like those. We may have to live in the same house, seeing you aren't gallant enough to spare me that, but underneath it all it's nothing but a situation forced on me by business demands. It's downright cruel of you to invade not only my business life, the career that means so much to me, but also my own home, destroying my privacy.'

Jonathan took her quickly by the upper arms, making use of the fact that she didn't want to disturb the children next door, and said, 'Fancy, talk like that between you and me! It's rather ridiculous, isn't it, when once we thought we'd spend the rest of our lives together? When we planned to share nights as well as days. When we planned to be one, in flesh *and* spirit. I was no end of a fool, wasn't I? Engaged for so short a time, then flying back to London so confident you'd follow me, live my life there. Women do still follow their men, even in these days. But not *you*. Your roots were too deep here. You set a place above the man you were supposed to love. Yes, it's a beautiful bay, perhaps more beautiful than any other . . . the very gates of heaven in sheer beauty as well as in its name, but you couldn't take separation from it, could you, Camilla Rose Hallows? You just didn't grow up. You didn't know that I'd planned that if you lived *my* life for a few years, proved to me that you loved *me*, as any man wants to be loved, set above all other people, all other places, I would have brought you back here.'

She said in a low, intense tone, 'Leave go of me. I can see through all this. That sounds very fine. You've found a reason for me giving you up—a bogus reason, as it happens. It saves your pride. I told you in my letter I thought it had all been one huge romantic mistake, that I couldn't marry you. But the real reason was that once you departed I didn't miss you at all, I simply stopped loving you, Jonathan Lemaire. It couldn't stand your absence. So what was it worth? Nothing.'

She'd had to say that. Because something, she didn't know what, held her back from flinging her knowledge of his dishonesty in his face.

He let her go so suddenly she almost fell back. He strode to the window, looked out on the last light fading in a steely shimmer above the waters of the Inlet. Then he came back to her, but didn't touch her this time, and said in a toneless voice, 'How strange. When your grandmother came to England, she told me she knew you still carried a torch for me. Or rather, she reverted to the legend of the old Kemp house at Kerikeri, and said, "She still has a lamp in the window for you." What do you think of that?'

Camilla swallowed. 'She couldn't be more mistaken. I didn't wish for your particular boat to come to this harbour again, Jonathan. There isn't any lamp in the window.'

There was a silence between them. Then suddenly he laughed and a confident ring sounded in it, to her dismay. 'But you know what it meant when the ships found no lamp in the window at Kerikeri, don't you? It didn't mean stand out to sea, don't come in. It meant "proceed with caution". That's exactly what I'll do, Camilla, I warn you.'

She said, on a whisper of sound, 'Then if you come to grief, don't blame me, Jonathan,' and ran out of the room, and downstairs to join the others.

She lay awake so long that night, wrestling with her emotions, willing them not to override her reason. It was one thing having willed Jonathan out of her life when he was thirteen thousand miles away, quite another coping with him right here. So many thoughts chased through her mind. Had he ever meant to come back again? Or had Grandmother's visit sparked it off? She was sure it was all tied up with business opportunity. The Lemaire business in London was a flourishing one, but Jonathan's father was in it and his three sons. Stephen and Randall were senior to Jonathan and he had probably chafed against being the youngest and saw this as a heaven-sent chance of becoming the male partner, possibly the dominant one, in another firm, giving him greater scope.

Camilla could imagine her grandmother, as was her

custom, coming straight to the point, saying: 'We need a man in the firm. I don't like the idea of Camilla running it on her own when I'm gone. How about it?' He'd evidently vetoed the idea of being given shares. Buying-in would give him a stronger hold, no matter what the future might bring. He could think that in time to come the situation might alter, strengthen his own position. That to become one of the family by marrying into it, as he'd thought to do once, would be the greatest gain of all. So he was pretending to himself that he'd never stopped caring!

Perhaps he'd always thought along those lines, even in those far-off, seeming idyllic days when they were engaged. Anyone capable of using underhand methods to take priceless, rare Maori artifacts out of their own land, away from their heritage of culture, could easily have had ulterior motives when it came to courting. Something in her cried out against the thought, something of remembered sweetness, when she had known not only love, but trust too. However, one wasn't as naïve and easily deceived now. A man's ambition might easily lead him towards a marriage that was not only attractive, but profitable. Expedient, if not a grand passion.

Good job she'd found him out. At first she'd not been able to believe it, had thought it no more than a coincidence that Mrs Moorie had been diddled out of that possession for just a fraction of its real value. But then Jonathan wouldn't have dreamed she'd have a friend in London at the very time Lemaire's sold the greenstone. She owed Dilys a great deal for that, yet how true it was, even unfair, that we rarely love those who destroy our illusions.

She tried to tell herself Dilys had meant nothing malicious when she'd written, 'It looks as if Jonathan didn't waste his time in New Zealand. How clever of him to pick it up for a song and smuggle it out. He's a really smart business man. He'll be good for you, because

you're rather too other-worldly, Camilla, to be really
successful.'

Even now Camilla felt sick to think of the discrepancy
in price between what Mrs Moorie had been paid and
what Lemaire's had realised. That was when she'd sent
the ruby ring back to Jonathan, terminating their engagement with never a hint of the real reason why.

Oddly enough, he mentioned Dilys the next day. Aunt
Rose had taken the children off their hands for a few
hours while they went into facts and figures, inspected
stock, all of it still seeming unreal to Camilla.

He picked up one of a set of Mary Gregory glasses,
with an exquisite painting of a child catching a butterfly,
outlined on the ruby glass. 'Remember your friend
Dilys, Camilla? She came into our showroom a few
weeks ago and wanted to purchase a set of these.' He
laughed. 'She had the nerve to think that because she
was a friend of yours she could probably get them at
cost price. I soon disabused her mind of that idea.'

'I'm sure you would,' said Camilla, 'you aren't one to
let sentiment interfere with profit.'

He looked at her sharply. 'Would *you*? For merely a
friend of a friend? Or more correctly a friend of an ex-
fiancée?'

She saw her grandmother's brows twitch together in
displeasure and said hastily, 'No, of course not. I was
endorsing your action. I think she had a nerve.
Incidentally, she must have changed a lot. She never
had a feeling for old things when she was here.'

Jonathan grinned. 'No, it wasn't for her. She'd fallen
for someone who has a lot of stuffy relations, according
to her, who go in for such things. She was going down
to Hampshire to stay with his mother, who collects glass,
and she thought a gift like that might make an impression. She was quite open about it. No thought that I
might despise her for such an attitude.'

Elinor said, 'You were lucky she didn't hang round

you or your people. She's one who uses people—always did. Her mother was the same. She was at school with Rose.'

His voice was dry. 'Oh, she did hang round after Camilla broke things off. She came in to utter sympathy and became a bally nuisance. Camilla will probably curl her lip and think me vain, but she really did have the idea of catching me on the rebound. She's not subtle and she bounced back time and again, but I finally made it very plain that I'd not then given up hope that Camilla might change her mind.'

There was a silence. When Camilla thought she could trust her voice she said, 'Is there any chance of keeping to business? I would prefer that.'

Elinor laughed, pure mischief in the sound. 'I have the most extraordinary feeling ... as if this isn't for real, but something I'm watching on a television screen.'

Camilla sighed. 'It certainly isn't for real. It's all airy-fairy nonsense. That happened five years ago. It's as dead as mutton. Let's get on with the things that really matter. Jonathan, I would appreciate your valuation of something in the packing-room that came in two days ago. Some of it I know is junk, some good. But there's some I'm not sure about. It's a deceased's estate and I'm glad it came to us. I was appalled to think how they might have got cheated had they sent it off to some secondhand shop in the city, or disposed of it at an auction. Come on over here.'

That night she slept well. She felt reasonably pleased that she had reduced their association to a business footing. When the children departed, they wouldn't be forced together, in that intimate sphere of substitute parents. She would go out more with her other friends, show Jonathan she had a life of her own, not entirely wrapped up in an old lady and an historical home. She must learn to be tough, to adapt to Jonathan's presence here, just as, long ago, she had adapted to his absence, through what had seemed then aeons of time and pain. At twenty you were vulnerable, a green girl. *Not now.*

Sleep was healing. She came down to start the breakfast, clear-eyed, the strands of gold-brown hair at her temples curling damply from her shower, elegant in a plain rose-coloured skirt, wrapped over at one side, slit at the other, and a filmy, cool floral blouse over it, in rose and grey and green. Against the brown throat lay a translucent rose-pink necklace, a treasure from the showroom. Her nails showed the same frosty pink.

Jonathan came in, a child on either hand. 'Hallie would like you to accompany me out to Galbraiths'. She feels Hester Galbraith will be glad to have news of London and London sales and appreciate some advice on what to go for. Hallie tells me she's delightful, with exquisite taste, and this is the dream of their lives, now her husband has retired, to own a house of such antiquity as this. Incidentally, she wants us to go the long way round, to drop off a frame for a Maori portrait at one of the small bays past Matauri Bay. What name did she say? Oh yes, to the Nukus. I guess you know them?'

'I'll say. I went to High School with Airini Nuku and since then she's become my best friend. But have you any idea how rough the road is, how far? The corrugations have to be seen to be believed ... or felt! And talk about dust! The surface is so ridgy that one man found his car juddering round and he finished up facing the opposite way, to his great amazement. He had no one in the back seat to hold it down, and it was a hot day, so his tyres had developed too much pressure.'

Jonathan said smoothly, 'And he was probably not taking the corrugations fast enough or slowly enough. I remember there are two safe speeds. And my car isn't exactly a Mini. It holds the road very well. You could also remember I had a lot of experience on your back country roads five years ago; I'm not exactly a new chum.' He paused, added, 'If you're dead set against the idea I'll go by myself. I've a fair idea from what Hallie told me that Mrs Galbraith might take several pieces from my shipment, and also that she had to take some of the chattels with the house and wants a price on them. But if you veto the trip I'll manage even if I don't know the local market yet.'

That did it. Camilla thought swiftly of old Forbes, the former owner, and his uncanny luck in ploughing up Maori artifacts, and said hastily, 'I'd better come, though I had other plans, but I like to see people getting a fair deal.'

The brows came down over the narrow dark eyes. 'Of course. That's the only way to run a business like ours. We're not like these fly-by-night salesmen dashing madly round the country, seeking whom they may devour and driving hard bargains. That's why I want you with me. You're *au fait* with local basic values and can estimate profitability. This is so very often a two-way business, buying from and selling to the same client.'

Camilla said slowly, 'Not only then does it apply, but when it's a case of buying only, we like to think they get a square deal. It mightn't mean a sensational profit, but it's how *we* run things.'

He tightened his lips, set his elbows on the breakfast-table and looked her straight in the eye. 'You *have* changed. Years ago you'd never have spoken like that. What is it? Have you developed the idea that all United Kingdom dealers are sharks, scouting round to buy family treasures from Colonial houses for a song and making fabulous profits?'

She regarded him steadily. 'Not all. Some. It *has* been known. Better for me to make it clear from the outset that Hallows House will continue its business on the same lines as my grandfather laid down. *And always must.*'

Jonathan said stiffly, 'You've met my own grand-parents. How could you consider them as any less upright than your own? Don't be absurd, Camilla! How——'

'You're two generations farther on. And we live in a permissive society, remember? Things are lax in many ways, and that lowering of standards could apply to business methods as well as human relationships. You know the jargon . . . the weakest to the wall, and you've got to be tough to survive in today's commercial jungle. I've heard it all. Well, those things don't apply here in Reikorangi. I merely thought I'd make it clear from the start.'

'You have—abundantly. Camilla, you can keep tabs on me. I realise it was a shock to you, your grandmother bringing me into the business like this. You were bound to resent it. But don't go looking for business practices that are near dishonesty, just to prove to Hallie that she made a mistake. Or making it so unpleasant for me that I'll clear off. I would like you to have known I was coming in, but your grandmother wouldn't hear of it.

'She was so strong on the point, she convinced me finally, made me remember that when I flew out to see you five years ago because I thought that ending an engagement by registered letter was no way at all, you upped and offed. How was I to know you wouldn't do it again and perhaps spoil the relationship between you and your grandmother?'

Camilla referred to this when they were on their way. 'Was that your only reason for not letting me know what was in the wind? The fact that it might upset things between Hallie and me?'

'Yes. It's not my way, as a rule, to go behind backs. I didn't last time, did I? I didn't fly out to surprise you. Maybe my mission wouldn't have been a failure if I had. So you have yourself to blame for this. Your grandmother could bear your absence then . . . even if only just . . . she's aged a lot since. I couldn't do it to her again.'

When Camilla didn't answer he said, 'Do you not

realise she fretted so much for you, I didn't dare prolong my visit? I had to return to London so you would come home to her.'

She was still silent.

This time his voice rasped. 'You have the air of not believing me. Is this possible? It used to be so different between us once. I hope you didn't think I should have chased you to Melbourne.'

Stung, she said, 'I was running *away* from you, not playing hard to get. I'd hoped my letter and the return of your ring would have ended it. I couldn't stand the thought of it starting up all over again.'

The narrow eyes rested on her briefly, then he turned back to the road. Camilla hated the derisive note in his voice. 'You were really afraid I'd mesmerise you into accepting me again.'

She copied his tone. 'How vain can a man get?'

He laughed shortly. 'Are men who get jilted likely to be vain?'

Surprisingly she found herself saying, 'Sorry, that was stupid.'

'Then why *did* you run?'

She considered that. 'Perhaps I was afraid of family pressure. Everyone was trying to marry us off, they were all so glad when we became engaged, shocked when I broke it off. A combination like that *can* make you feel a match would be ideal—the grandson of one old school friend marrying the granddaughter of another, and both in the antique trade. Quite a formidable combination for a girl of twenty. Especially one who'd been brought up mainly with one generation of family missing, my mother and father.'

The next moment she was saying, 'Jonathan, what are you stopping for?' He turned to look at her and in a fleeting moment she realised that the line of jaw she'd thought of years ago as clear-cut was really aggressive. But all he said, waving a hand, was, 'I've not seen that view for so long don't you think it's worth five minutes of our time?'

From the crest of the hill they could see the immensely bitten-in expanse of the Reikorangi Inlet. Countless bays and miniature headlands curved round a sheet of azure water to merge into the greater gulf of the Bay of Islands. So many islands, each a little world of its own. Jonathan said, 'Out,' and, bemused, Camilla obeyed him.

They walked to the weathered wooden rails that formed an ancient gate into a sweeping hill-paddock grazed on by russet-and-white Hereford steers. Out on the Kerikeri and Reikorangi waters small sailing craft tacked to and fro, launches with tourists aboard headed out towards the open sea and Cape Brett where they would be taken on the breathtaking venture through the Hole in the Rock, fishing launches cruised at a lower speed. Cottonwool clouds scattered and amassed against the blue of the sky. There must have been half a dozen larks singing in the sky above, too high to be even specks.

'Larks singing,' said Jonathan. 'Camilla, do you remember that day you said dreamily that the sound of larks singing was the symbol of our happiness?'

Startled, because she had thought he was absorbed in the beauty of the seascape below, Camilla turned to him and then had to drop her eyes before his burning gaze. The wind blew a strand of hair across her face. He put a hand out, took it, smoothed it back behind her ear, felt for the tortoiseshell comb at that side, pulled it out and brought it forward so the errant tendril stayed in place. She willed herself to look unaware of his touch.

He said, 'It was that day on Silver Head. We'd taken the launch there and climbed the cliff to the top where the tussocks were all blown silver in the sun and we promised there to marry each other. There were daisies in the tussock, and the gnarled old *ngaios* on the cliffs were in bloom. Like daphne flowers, you said. Some of them fell on your hair. After I'd said my piece and you'd promised to marry me, we sat on that fallen tree and the larks sang on and the breakers crashed at the foot of the cliffs, and we planned a lifetime together. You were very sweet—I mean the *young* Camilla was very sweet. It didn't seem to me that she was under *any* pressure from her family or mine. Perhaps I was a romantic young fool, but I thought there was an inevitability about our marrying. It seemed so right.'

He continued, 'There were other hours. I'm sure I wasn't mistaken in your responsiveness. You'll recall there were hours when we had to be guarded lest our emotions swamp us. I had to go back to London before too long, but I knew that soon I'd return to marry you, bringing grandparents and parents with me, then carry you off to all the enchantment of the Old World, feeling it would delight you, to see where the Colonial treasures you knew so well had come from in the manor houses and cottages a century ago. But it all fell to bits in a bolt from the blue.'

This was potent stuff. Old longings and desires rose within her. She felt infuriated that her physical feeling for him should so betray her. She kept her voice as cool as possible. 'I think it's easy to look back to early idyllic days, Jonathan, but I doubt if we can ever find our way back. You're not really asking me to believe that you stayed devoted to my memory ever since? That you never took another girl out?'

He made an impatient gesture. 'Of course not. When I arrived in New Zealand to find out what had gone wrong, all those years ago, and found you hadn't even stayed to see me, I was so furious that when I did get back to England, after seeing how miserable Hallie was, I made up my mind to put you right out of my life. I felt you weren't worth agonising over. I kidded myself for a time that I was succeeding, in other girls' company, but it didn't mean a thing. I got a flat, tried to live it up. It didn't work.'

Camilla permitted herself a curl of the lip. 'So now

you kid yourself that you nursed your sorrow till now. Oh dear! But you waited till my grandmother arrived with a very advantageous offer before you decided ... or did she decide that for you? That you ought to have another shot?'

This time Jonathan didn't answer. White lines compressed themselves about his lips and nostrils. Camilla said, 'No need to look so outraged. Tell me and tell me true ... *would* you have come back to try again if Gran hadn't come to London and proposed this?'

'Actually no, because——'

She held her hand up. 'Leave it at that, Jonathan. It's honest. The excuse might not be.'

'I can well imagine you wouldn't believe it. You'd think it was more of my imagining, my self-deceit. So I *will* let it go. The young Camilla I loved *would* have done. She had a habit of believing people, and believing in them. The new Camilla does neither.'

'The young Camilla was gullible. I'm certainly not, and I don't just care that you seem to prefer the naïve young one.'

'I certainly preferred her to what you are now. *This one I don't even like.*'

No one would have known that that hit her like a blow in the diaphragm. She said calmly, 'Then stop all this silly business recalling courting days. Recalling moods and hours ... they were only passing attractions. And do let's get on with today's business. I don't mind stopping to admire a view, but I do object to wasting time quarrelling. Let's get off the personal.'

'Can we ever get off the personal? You and me?'

'Well, if we're not going to, we've a very exhausting time ahead. Don't try me too far, Jonathan. I skipped once.'

'You wouldn't now. Not with Hallie at the age she is. And knowing that this time I'm here to stay.'

Camilla said, with bitterness, 'You have me in a cleft stick. How very gallant!'

He laughed. 'Well, isn't it supposed to be all fair in love and war?'

She said slowly, 'It isn't love, so it must be war. I've heard of strife between business rivals, but *I've* got to suffer it within the family business. It just isn't fair. What good can come of an association where one member doesn't even like the other as you just said, I don't know.'

Jonathan's tone was still amused. 'Then you know what you must do . . . revert to the nice girl you used to be, one I could like and admire, and all could be well. And it isn't war.'

'And it can't be love.'

'Why not?'

She could have stamped her foot, but didn't. She said, on a sigh, 'It isn't even liking. You just said so.'

He turned her round to face him, holding her by her elbows. 'Camilla, you aren't stupid. You're crazy . . . all mixed-up, and wilful and blind, but not stupid. You know perfectly well we can love people without liking and admiring them. That's why some marriages don't last. There's got to be love *and* liking. I remember my mother once saying . . . immediately after a spanking . . . that when I was naughty she still loved me but didn't like me. Not for me any love-hate relationship. I'd want trust and liking and respect too.'

She resisted the temptation to fling at him that that was exactly what she couldn't give him . . . trust and respect. She got back into the car, said over her shoulder, 'This is a business trip. Let's get on with it.'

CHAPTER THREE

SHE hated his imperturbability for all that, the way he could converse as if none of this had occurred. 'Hallie put me in the picture as far as Hester Galbraith's background was concerned. I take it she married Captain Galbraith when he was on shore leave in England during the war, and they had a home in Auckland when he returned to merchant shipping; that they always loved Northland, spent their holidays up here when their family were small, and now have decided to retire here. How come they're able to afford the sort of antiques she's talking about?'

'It's rather lovely. They had a holiday cottage up here—the sort of thing many people have, adequate, but only just. Then a remote connection of hers, in Britain, a recluse who had shunned all his relations all his life, but had had a soft spot for her mother, left them a considerable sum of money. This property became available ... one they'd often coveted when cruising around on vacation. It's one of the most beautiful spots on Whangaroa Harbour, and that's saying something. A tiny bay, overhung with pohutukawa trees so at Christmas it's rimmed with scarlet blossom, completely private, yet manageable for a couple their age and with their interests. They have two passions, gardening and boating. Old Forbes ran sheep on the outer property, but that adjoined his son's farm, so he took over that part of it. Hester and John are building chalets for the families of their own children for holidays. Hester's very open about her affairs, said her relation left them enough to buy Arapito and they put the money from their Auckland property into the chalets. That way they all share, and her sons and daughter can bring their children whenever they like, and it's not too much for the grandparents.'

'I like that,' said Jonathan. 'Generosity and affection but freedom too. Very understanding.'

'M'm, not all relations achieve that. They create bonds out of family love—and let you know they hold the reins.'

He didn't answer. When next he spoke it was just to say, 'I liked the way Hester Galbraith said the name of their bay, Arapito. As if it meant a lot to her. What does it mean?'

'It means the end of the path. *Ara* is path, *pito* is end. I think in full it's Whanga-o-arapito, the bay or harbour where the road ends. Beyond it the cliffs are too steep.'

'So it's fitting. Journey's end for them.'

Once more Camilla was assailed by regret—an unwelcome feeling. Journey's end for two people still in love with each other. What would her own journey's end be like? In whose company?

'I'm going to go down that corkscrew road into Matauri Bay,' announced Jonathan.

'There's no need. We turn left just before that. It will make us late.'

'Isn't the Bay of Islands the place where time stands still? Where you get away from the rat-race?'

'If you're on holiday, yes. No point in going there today.'

'Not to you, perhaps, but there is to me. I might recapture the magic of the first time I saw it. I'll never forget the entrancing glimpse of the Cavalli Islands lying out from that curving bay, from about halfway down.'

There were no other cars on the road, so they were able to stop to do justice to it, the solitude and the immensity. But suddenly Jonathan said harshly, 'What a mistake . . . beauty beyond belief, I know, but it wasn't only the scenery made it magic that day. I'll just turn at the bottom of the hill. I don't want to go down to the sea. It'd be a waste to linger.'

Camilla had to clasp her hands tightly on her rose-pink lap to stop them shaking. In silence they regained the top road and began to skirt all the darling little bays, each of them dotted with tiny islands, mute testimony to headlands eroded by the sea millions of years ago. Not a word was spoken till they came to the miniature bay where only the Nukus lived, their farm sprawling up the hills behind, their house built across it, with wide patios above the rock steps that led down to the sea where their boats were moored. Airini came running out in a white sun-dress, laughing a welcome to them, her parents not far behind her, so Jonathan and Camilla instantly became normal, and were persuaded to have morning tea at a table on the patio canopied with a gay sun-umbrella.

'How could I have stayed away so long?' said Jonathan lightly. 'I must have been mad.'

Airini flicked a quick look at Camilla's face and looked away out to sea again. She wouldn't utter a word that might embarrass them, Camilla knew. When Laura and Charles Nuku took Jonathan down the steps to look at a crayfish pot, Camilla said, 'Thanks, Airini, for taking it so naturally. It's not on again. It's just a business arrangement Gran made with the Lemaires when she was in London—she thinks we need a man in the business and, heaven help me, picks on my ex-fiancé.'

Airini laughed lightly. 'Grandmothers can be the very devil, I know. Mine thinks it's a disgrace that I'm twenty-six and not married. I'm so tired of them inviting all and sundry for holidays here ... as many bachelors as possible. So I escaped to Whakatane to my cousins there last time she was up to her tricks, and ...' dimples showed for a moment, 'I met my fate there. But I'm not telling them yet. If I do they'll fix the date for me.'

Camilla laughed delightedly, and on the heels of her laughter the other three came back and they piled into the car again. Nevertheless silence once more sat heavily upon them even though there was so much to comment

on ... remnants of primeval forests, pockets of evergreen bush starred with the symmetrical bursts of tree-
ferns that flourished wherever they could find a foot-
hold. There were stud cattle farms, with bright gardens
where bottle-brushes blazed scarlet, bougainvillea
cascaded over rocks and trellises in cerise and purple,
wild arum lilies edged the drives and bird-of-paradise
flowers gave the impression that if you clapped your
hands, they'd fly away.

Suddenly they came to Whangaroa, the Long
Harbour, in all its scintillating blue. They turned away
from the little port and began winding round bays and
inlets till the road climbed high above Arapito.

The pohutukawas deepened the shadows at the
water's edge, but across the far side the house itself was
bathed in sunshine, because the garden had been created
in a clearing with a magnificent backdrop of evergreen
bush, or forest. It had beautiful lines, with a steep roof
intersected with dormers that looked like eyes peeping
out and keeping guard over the bay beneath. Across the
harbour was St Paul's Rock jutting out of the verdure
on the summit of the hill above Whangaroa Township
and on this side, St Peter's Rock.

The garden about it blazed in the November weather,
early summer in New Zealand with all the flowers of an
English summer plus heady datura lilies, in white and
pink, the flaming scarlets and rich purples of the bou-
gainvilleas spilling from arches and trellises, oleanders,
orange bignonias, gaudy melon flowers, banana passionfruit climbers with clover-pink starlike flowers and
pendulous green fruit forming, and the true passionfruit
vines were rosetted with palest cream and heliotrope
feathery circles. Hibiscus opened great crimson and yellow
and pink cups, and Livingstone daisies blazed against dry
earth under standard fuchsias of every hue and shape.

Above it all tuis twanged their woodland harps, and
chuckled gutturally as they mocked the bellbirds' more
silvery chimes.

Jonathan looked and sighed. 'They've come to safe harbourage in their later years.'

Instinctively Camilla responded to that faint hint of envy. 'But they knew rough seas first. Imagine loving someone who was in the U-boat-infested Atlantic. He survived being torpedoed three times, I believe.'

'Of course. But perhaps it taught them true values. They knew that all that mattered eventually, was to be together again, and to make the most of every hour. Every moment. Not to waste time.'

Something in Camilla shrank from the bitterness in his tone. For the first time ever Camilla was visited by a sense of guilt. She had never doubted till now that she had done the right thing. Another sensation succeeded it. Was it . . . could it possibly be that this amalgamation of the Lemaires' grandson with the firm of Hallows wasn't just a fortuitous business deal? Did he still have a remnant of their former feelings for each other, deep within him? Till now she had thought he was deceiving himself.

She brushed the thought impatiently aside. Whatever happened she mustn't let herself be gulled. Her one-time idol, her one-time dear love had proved to have feet of clay. Don't gild the clay, Camilla, don't let yourself even think it looks like pure gold. Fakes always show up, sooner or later.

It wasn't as if she'd just gone on the evidence of the clipping about Lemaire's selling that Maori artifact. She'd been so reluctant to believe it, so willing to make up her mind it had found its way into Lemaire's sale-rooms from another source, an unscrupulous source, that she'd gone across to old Mrs Moorie's and said to her straight out, 'Mrs Moorie, I want you to tell me something. Did Jonathan Lemaire visit you here just before he went back to London? Did he buy anything from you?'

Old Mrs Moorie had laughed and nodded. 'He did

and all! And a fine to-do there was when my son and his wife found out what I'd done. It ought to have been kept in the family, they said. But I needed the money. Tom, he said he'd have given me the same amount just to have the *mere* stay in New Zealand. But he wouldn't have, you know. He only had to wait till I died and it'd have been his. So why part with his money? Funny, isn't it, the store they set by these things these days? Time was when they wouldn't ha' cared. And Tom's one generation farther than me from the Maori ancestor who owned it. He's about seven-eighths *pakeha* and one-eighth Maori, but it's a dominant eighth.'

Camilla had managed to say, 'I think that's a good thing, Mrs Moorie, and it's not uncommon to feel kinship with one particular ancestor. Like me, I feel I have the strongest ties with my ancestor who built Hallows House . . . the first missionary carpenter in Reikorangi. I've often a strange feeling, when I handle his walking-stick and his hammer, that I feel his hand round mine. Why shouldn't Joe feel that way about Tawhiri?'

Her head had been whirling, her thoughts chaotic. The fact that Jonathan hadn't told her proved he knew she wouldn't approve. It wouldn't have seemed so bad had he come back, displayed his acquisition and said, 'I managed to get this for a reasonable price. The old lady was very satisfied. She needed the cash and *we'll* reap a good profit.'

She wouldn't have allowed him to take it out of New Zealand. Perhap's he'd known that. She would have made him see the enormity of it, kidding an old lady, almost in her dotage, to part with such a treasure—a jade weapon, handmade in the not-so-distant stone age of the early New Zealanders. But he had known it was wrong and had kept it a secret, and Camilla couldn't take it. Oh, they could do without that kind of business craftiness in the firm of Hallows. They stood for everything of integrity and trust throughout the length and breadth of New Zealand and Australia.

Now they were down the steep winding drive that led through the dimness of the bush to the plateau on which the Galbraiths' house was built. The Captain and Hester came out swiftly on to the long verandah edged with iron lace.

Jonathan exclaimed, 'Heavens, I expected a white-haired old couple! I suppose mentioning they were grandparents did that. What a handsome pair! There's quite a bit of copper in her hair still, and he's got a look of the late Earl Mountbatten.'

'So he has. I always felt he looked familiar. We've only known them the last two or three years.'

Hester's pleasure spilled over in her greeting, as she held out her hands to both of them, squeezing Jonathan's and kissing Camilla's cheek. 'This is just too marvellous! Mr Lemaire ... or may I call you Jonathan?—I just can't believe I've got a member of that famous family of art dealers at this far-off spot. This is Noel, my husband. I lived just out of Portsmouth most of the time during the war and when it was over we had a farewell week in London. We had very little money, but Noel bought me the first antique we ever owned ... at Lemaire's. It was a Victorian work-table with a pouch beneath it for embroidery silks. I still use it. It seemed quite crazy to buy such a thing when we hadn't even the bare necessities for the home we had to set up, but it was somehow a grand gesture to the things of old England that had survived the blitz.'

Jonathan nodded. 'I like that. One has to be practical in most things, but we have a need, most of us, I suppose, to gratify something not practical. At least that's what I find in our trade. Like a Vicar's wife I dealt with just before leaving home. She was a teetotaller ... but fell in love with a set of Venetian glass decanter and liqueur glasses. An aunt had left her a small legacy. The Vicar wanted her to have something quite unnecessary and beautiful, and she'd admired it in our showrooms for over a year, he said.'

'Oh, you *are* a kindred spirit,' said Hester happily. 'Come on in, and before we show you round, or talk business in any way, you must have a cup of morning tea. I made fresh cheese scones and cream kisses. I do hope you've a good appetite and aren't dieting or anything, Camilla.'

Jonathan turned and surveyed Camilla from top to toe. 'I can personally guarantee she hasn't put on an ounce in five years.'

Noel said, 'Oh, have you always known each other? Mrs Hallows just said she'd been fortunate enough to be able to take one of the Lemaire grandsons into the business and that he was putting in goods in lieu of capital. Have you been to London, Camilla?'

To her annoyance she felt warmth in her cheeks. She shook her head and smiled. 'No, I hope to go some day. Jonathan's grandmother was a New Zealander, and a schoolfriend of Gran's. There's always been some going and coming between the two families. Jonathan came out with his grandmother to pay mine a visit when he was twelve.'

Jonathan grinned, that devilish grin she knew only too well. 'But that doesn't explain the five-year gap I just referred to, Camilla. I came out here then, Hester, and got myself engaged to this girl here. But in her case absence didn't make the heart grow fonder, and she broke it off. Stupid thing to do ... the two grandmamas thought it was like something out of a Victorian romance ... you know, it all went with antiques. However, there are other bonds than holy matrimony, and now we've settled for business ones. Haven't we, Camilla?'

Hester burst out laughing, 'Well, I must say you treat it all very sensibly. No hard feelings, I can see. Much better than letting me drop clangers all over the place, which I'm rather prone to do. Let's have our scones while they're still warm, then we'll prowl. You can evaluate the things I don't want to keep, even if you don't want to buy, and we'll work in a bathe before lunch.'

Camilla said, 'Oh, I didn't bring anything with me, so——'

Jonathan interrupted her. 'Sorry, I forgot to tell you. Hester rang about that. Aunt Rose put your togs and a towel in the boot of the car.'

High-handed hound! thought Camilla to herself.

As they dived and splashed about in the deep emerald green water off the boat jetty in this private bay, Jonathan said, 'This really is the life. Combining work and pleasure ... not much scope for such diversity in London.'

Camilla said lightly, treading water, 'But a hundred other compensations ... you could visit historical spots in your lunch hour, for instance. Wander through Green Park and imagine you were back in Regency days. Haunt Fleet Street, wander up the Square where Dr Johnson lived.'

Hester cried delightedly, 'Oh, even though you've not been there you know it by hearsay.'

Camilla looked rueful. 'Grandmother knows it so well I feel I do.'

Jonathan said, 'She ought to have visited there long since. But she will before long, now, I'm sure.'

Camilla surprised a knowing gleam in Hester Galbraith's eye, and said quickly, 'He means that now we've another partner, I'll be able to leave Grandmother more easily.'

Jonathan splashed water at Camilla. 'She ought to have come this time when Hallie visited us. Aunt Rose could easily have managed it with Wilma. But she was too chicken.'

Too chicken! Meaning she was afraid to meet him. What a nerve, what a colossal nerve! She dived deeply, seized his ankles and pulled him under. Noel did the same to Hester. They all came up, laughing, spluttering, and Noel said, 'This sort of thing makes me feel younger. It's good not to have the little ones round ...

when we have to underline the fact that horseplay in the water is dangerous.'

They came up to a lunch that had been cooking itself in the oven, some sort of glamorous seafood concoction and a salad, quickly prepared, plus a pavlova filled with whipped cream and the new season's luscious Northland strawberries.

Then they got down to business. It was slightly galling that Hester and Noel seemed to automatically defer to Jonathan. As if being male (which was ridiculous in these days) made him the senior partner. Or perhaps it was because as he came from the hub of the universe, they felt he was more knowledgeable.

Certainly he knew to the last small item what was in that container on the ship forging her way to New Zealand, and had a flair for knowing what would suit this beautiful house. He said, 'The mistake that some people make when they set about restoring a house like this, which they're going to live in, not open to the public, is to try to keep it all in the one period. Now Hallows Green—the public part—has to be kept to furniture that was in keeping then. No good introducing later stuff. But in a house like this, that's been lived in for nearly a hundred and fifty years, it must be an authentic revelation of the tastes of several generations. A house is never a static entity, it grows and develops just as the people who've lived in it did. It's a mistake to have everything Victorian or Edwardian. And of course much of the stuff that the early settlers brought out, especially the wealthier ones, was Regency and Georgian, even older in silverware and porcelain.

'Some of this stuff that belongs to the 1920s, I agree, must go. It has a certain value, but was very utility. However, some of the smaller pieces should be retained, even so. What does go will make room for some stuff I think you'll like from what's on the water. The pioneer family probably had some similar things and later occupants sold them for a song to make room for this less worthy stuff.'

Camilla could see how impressed the Galbraiths were by all this, and because she'd never before suffered a single pang of jealousy, she tried to subdue her stab of resentment. But Jonathan turned to her and said, 'Camilla, I don't know the local demand for this, but you will. Will we be best to try to sell these rejects ourselves, or find somewhere to dispose of them? . . . I suppose there'll be places in Auckland that deal more in this period, are there?'

She felt a warmth of gratitude invade her. She said, 'There are, but I know a couple of small places in Northland itself where they specialise in 1920s stuff. Even go in for selling clothing of that period, long ropes of beads, and so on. Much easier for Noel and Hester if we handle it than if they try to dispose of it all themselves. That particular sideboard, for instance, is quite a good selling type, and those two tables.' She turned to the Galbraiths. 'That would leave room for that chiffonier Jonathan spoke about . . . and perhaps the mahogany bureau bookcase . . . if you fall for them.'

Jonathan came in, 'We have something back at the showroom I'd love you to see quite soon. It would be ideal in that corner over there . . . look, step back here. Look through that open archway into that tiny passage with the windows on the left-hand side. On the right, at the far end, before you turn off through that door, you could have this glorious corner cupboard. It's a very fine piece, with a simple yet elegant impedimenta top, a leaded glass showcase, and beneath that, repeating the curve, is a very fine cupboard, inset with an oval panel of exquisitely grained wood. Camilla found it at a sale where it was almost lost sight of among much more prosaic stuff and had it beautifully restored. It's a gem. It would take the eye along the passage, making an extension of the room and a pleasing vista.' Camilla's resentment vanished.

On the way home, by another route, mostly tarsealed,

she said, rather diffidently, 'Jonathan, thank you for bringing me to the forefront this afternoon. I'll be candid—I was feeling as if I were being relegated to very much the junior partner.'

She saw the naturally olive skin of his cheek crease as he smiled. He glanced at her briefly, the narrow brown eyes glinting with amusement. 'Good for you, Camilla. You sound more like yourself, a little grudging perhaps, as if it goes against the grain to give the devil his due, yet you're so fundamentally fair you feel you must. I know exactly how you must be feeling. I've so often felt very much junior to my brothers, though not the last year or two. Grandpa saw to that. He told Steve and Randall I'd caught up and passed what they knew about antiques . . . at my age. It made a difference, yet it was Grandpa who was keen for me to come out here, so it wasn't just that he was wanting to extend my training for his own firm that he insisted my brothers gave me a fair go. Of course he's always had a——' He compressed his lips and said no more.

Without thinking, Camilla, who had been avoiding personal contact as much as possible, put her hand on his bare forearm and said, 'He's always had . . . what? I hate it when people break off just when they're about to say something you think might be interesting.'

She thought he looked rueful. That seemed odd, because he was—or had been since he came back—so sure of himself.

She said curiously, 'Why don't you want to tell me?'

He considered it. 'Why? Because you might feel it exerted even more pressure upon you.'

'Pressure to bring about what?'

'You won't like it. To bring about reconciliation between you and me,' he said simply.

She'd better not appear to resent that or he'd never tell her what he'd been going to say. Unthinkingly she left her hand on his arm.

Jonathan drew the car into the side of the road and

turned to face her a little. His other hand came up to cover hers. She left it there, for the same reason showing no resentment.

To prod him she said, a line etched between her brown brows, her eyes fixed on his, 'There's always been pressure to bring us together, before our engagement, and then afterwards, when I broke it. You know, Jonathan, you and I haven't really had much of a chance—to live our own lives, I mean. My grandmother and yours were such bosom pals, inseparables. Then your grandmother took that trip to England, fell in love with your grandpa, and the one cloud on her happiness was that she would be separated by half a world from her boon companion. But as the businesses of both prospered, they were able to take trips to see each other. I think from the very time your mother brought you out here when you were twelve, the two friends made up their minds that it would be idyllic if we married. So there's always been some pressure. So what's new about that? . . . Oh, you said Grandpa, didn't you, not one of the grandmamas. Why?'

His hand tightened on hers. 'I don't suppose you'd ever guess. I wouldn't have myself if it hadn't been more or less revealed to me in the strangest way. Grandpa came out as a young man to marry Kathy, and to take her back with him. Only somehow, he and your grandmother seemed to recognise each other for ideal the moment they met. There was never any thought of backing out. It was unthinkable to them both, They had only one brief half-hour or so when they admitted it to each other, then carried on.'

Her sherry-brown eyes looked into his almost black ones, seeking to find out if this indeed was truth. Her lips parted. 'The poor darlings! How—how on earth did you find out?'

Jonathan said slowly, 'I don't want to sound reproachful about this . . . but it was in the rather halcyon period between my going back to London, and you breaking off our engagement. That might sound odd, to call it halcyon when I was so far away from you, but I knew it wouldn't be for long. I was living with my grandparents, and Grandma went to look after her daughter in Northumberland when she broke an ankle. Grandpa picked up some virus, and was quite delirious for one whole night. I thought he was going off his rocker when he insisted on having his pocket-watch put into his hands, but I humoured him.

'He had it in a container similar to that one Prince Albert had attached to their bedhead in Osborne House—his favourite antique. I put it into his hands, and to my great surprise he opened a little compartment I'd never known existed, and I found myself gazing at a picture of your grandmother cut out of one of the wedding photos—in her bridesmaid's dress. In a tone of great satisfaction he muttered: "Sweet and true. Always," and then went into a fairly natural sleep. It scared seven bells out of me, though. I thought it sounded like Hail and Farewell. By next day the medication had done its work and he was quite lucid. He wouldn't let me get Grandma back. That night he asked me if he'd really handled his watch, and opened the back, or had he dreamed it? I thought it best to say he had.

'So he told me. He also said how happy he'd been with Grandma, and that your grandmother had made a good marriage too. He said it had been just a springtime idyll between the two of them. But he liked to remember it. I said I thought it was a bit risky keeping that photo there—couldn't bear the thought of Grandma being hurt if she found it. He showed me how foolproof it was, but conceded that it would be a pity, and he gave me the whole thing. I put it into safe deposit. He told Grandma he'd intended leaving it to me and thought I might as well have it now. He told me our engagement made him very happy.'

Camilla said, 'And you've never told anyone till now?'

'No. Of course I'd intended to tell you when we were married.'

She said slowly, 'I'm so glad they didn't make a mess of things. That Kathy and Elinor's friendship remained unclouded.'

Jonathan nodded. 'No strain on Kathy, of course, but Elinor really deserved that tribute . . . sweet and true.'

A silence fell between them that made Camilla immediately conscious of her hand on his arm, of the coarse black hairs under her fingers, of his hand covering hers. She went to draw away.

A flash came into the eyes so close to hers. 'Oh, no you don't,' he said. 'I'm all for recapturing the past. *Like this.*'

It was very hard to free oneself without a scuffle, especially when confined by a seat-belt. Besides, his fingers, forcing up her chin, were like steel. He gave a strange laugh . . . was it exultant, or merely amused at himself, or teasing? It was only afterwards she tried to analyse it. Because the next moment she was incapable of thought. Jonathan's lips came down on hers, just as she had remembered them, cool at first, tender, then more passionate. Not demanding, but seeking.

He lifted his mouth about half an inch from hers, then kissed her lightly on her cheeks, her forehead, waking old memories, using the old familiar pattern of caresses so that she instinctively closed her eyes as he came to kiss her eyelids, but when he came to the hollow in her throat, she drew away from him, brought her hands up on to his shoulders and said huskily, 'Jonathan . . . please . . . no . . . I can't get away from you with this damned belt on . . . so please! No more!'

Surprisingly, he did stop. But he chuckled again, maddeningly. He put his slightly rough cheek against hers, said, 'And here was I thinking that the sentimental little story of our forebears might have softened you!'

She didn't reply. He was too near, too dear. And he

wasn't to be trusted. His head, left against hers in that old familiarity, made her want to put her hand up to cradle it, but she wouldn't.

He could feel her breast rising and falling against him, mark her quickening breathing. He lifted his head, his breath was warm on her face, his eyes twinkling. 'It was nice, wasn't it? Some people think "nice" is an inadequate word. I don't. That describes what we've just had—nice. Don't you think so?' His lips twitched. 'Okay, Camilla Rose, I can see you're wearing an expression like an outraged Victorian whose beau has just complimented her upon her ankles. Well, it all goes with our trade, that's for sure. No wonder you're such a success with antiques!'

A car swept past them, hooting derisively. 'Now see what you've done,' said Camilla wrathfully. 'They've taken us for a canoodling couple . . . and this is such a small world . . . and your car is so noticeable. If we get back to find those people in the showroom, I'll kill you, Jonathan Peregrine Lemaire!'

Laughing, he drove off.

Camilla had to fight drowsiness. She wasn't going to drop off, and have her head slide towards Jonathan's shoulder. It had been a long day, and the sense of well-being that pervaded her had nothing whatever, she told herself, to do with the fact that she'd been kissed. It was merely the effect, common enough, of sun and sea and the open air. By dint of stern control she kept awake till they reached home. It was well after their usual dinner-hour and twilight was deepening a little. Aunt Rose would have put the children to bed and left a light meal for them. Grandmother would be sitting in her deep wing chair in its faded pastel brocades, reading or watching TV.

Camilla knew she would look at her differently, seeing the young Elinor, in her bridesmaid's finery, making the best of things, as she had made the best of life, building a fine marriage, even surmounting the loss of her son,

Camilla's father, with fortitude, and surrounding the little girl with laughter and joy. If she had wept, she had done it in privacy. For a moment Camilla was swept with a longing that things could have been different, that Jonathan had never diddled an old lady out of a family treasure, for a large profit, that she and the grandson of the young Elinor's true love could have given them the happiness of knowing their descendants were united.

Jonathan ran the Jaguar into the spare lean-to of the old stables. Together they came round the shell-path to the front verandah, and as they turned the corner, heard the creak of the picket-gate and the crunch of other feet down there. As the figure passed between two bushes, Camilla exclaimed with a gasp of dismay, 'Oh, heaven help us . . . it's the dilly Edie . . . do you remember her? And she won't know you're here. She's been in Whangarei for a couple of days.'

'Let's give her something to think about,' said Jonathan, and took her hand.

Edie was too near for Camilla to wrench it away. She came round the plum-coloured rhododendron and stopped dead, mouth open. Jonathan and Camilla, hands clasped, here in Reikorangi!

She closed her mouth, swallowed, then exclaimed, 'I can't believe it! Is it really you, Jonathan Lemaire? After all this time?'

He was laughing. 'It really is. The very same. And five years almost to the day.'

Edie was still boggling. 'Then it's on again!' she gasped.

Camilla was really at a loss for words. She must be definite, she must disabuse Edie's mind of such a thing once and for all, or she'd have it all over Reikorangi that the engagement was resumed.

But she wasn't quick enough. Jonathan spoke, his voice full of mocking regret. 'Alas, no,' he said, 'at least, *not yet!*'

Edie, in her surprise, had grasped at a long rope of pearls she had twisted and knotted round her neck. The string gave way, and the pearls cascaded to the crushed shells of the path. Edie gasped again, with dismay this time, and fell to her knees to try to pick them up. Camilla said, 'I'll leave you to help get that lot together, Jonathan . . . you're so gallant,' and she turned.

He said quickly, subduing a chuckle, 'Of course. I'll just get something to put them in, though, perhaps a saucer,' put his hand under her elbow and scooped her on to the verandah and through the open door, where Grandmother was tatting.

Camilla turned on him. 'I *will* kill you yet. Fancy giving Edie an answer like that! You idiot!'

Her grandmother surveyed them placidly. 'Dear me, Camilla, are you still taking offence?'

'Not all the time she isn't,' said Jonathan. 'Look, Hallie . . . the proof of that lies in the fact that she's got no lipstick left.' He held up a hand as if to ward off a blow from Camilla and added to her: 'You know you oughtn't to speak in superlatives *all* the time. Having threatened to kill me, you now have no worse fate for me in which to express yourself. Okay, I'm on my way to get this saucer . . . and you're coming to help me pick up those blasted pearls.'

CHAPTER FOUR

CAMILLA refused point-blank. 'I'll see to our tea. And watch what you say.' But heaven only knew if he'd heed her warning. Edie, of course, was irrepressible. Camilla came in with the plates of curried salmon and hard-boiled egg slices Aunt Rose had left for them, to hear Edie, as she entered with Jonathan bearing the saucer of pearls, say: 'Well, Elinor, it's a wonder you didn't take to your bed again, with the shock of having Jonathan arrive like this.'

Elinor's lips twitched. 'But that's why I *was* in bed ... getting my strength up for his arrival. It was no shock to me—I arranged it. The one who got the shock was Camilla, but she's rallied quite well.'

'She certainly seems to have done just that! I could scarcely believe my eyes ... coming round the path hand in hand!'

Elinor took it very calmly. 'Well, they weren't likely to stay at daggers drawn.'

Camilla said in as offhand a tone as she could manage, 'I feel about five years old, being discussed like this. Jonathan, will you have this on a tray on your knee, or——'

'We'll have it at this small table over here. Much more comfortable. And we'll want something for afters ... I don't know about you, but I'm starving. Nothing like the combination of sun, sea and sand to stimulate one's appetite. How about some of those currant and honey cakes?'

Edie said eagerly, 'Oh, you've been having a day off ... to get to know one another all over again?'

Camilla just had to put a stop to that. 'We certainly didn't. We bought a whack of stuff and sold—potentially—a good deal of the stuff Jonathan shipped out as part of the price of his partnership. But it was to the Galbraiths at Arapito and they insisted on a bathe before lunch—a novelty to Jonathan, but run of the mill to me.'

'You're being blasé,' Jonathan criticised. 'It takes a Londoner to appreciate all this. It's wasted on you, my girl.'

She could have choked him. Wasted on her? Her passionate love of this, her own lovely corner of a lovely land, swept over her . . . her eyes flickered to the scene below, the tree-girt inlet patched here and there with the rose-pink of the afterglow, the gleaming white hulls and masts of little craft, hardly rocking at their moorings, the white splash of the waterfall that was the river taking joyous leaps into the salt waters below . . . no, she was never blasé, and that devil of a Jonathan knew it. He caught her eye and grinned unrepentantly, holding out his cup for a refill.

He was sweet to Edie, patient with all her aimless questions, able to keep up with the way she darted from one subject to another. You could tell he'd lived a lot with older people. He even said, lifting their dishes on to a tea-trolley, 'I'll just wheel these out, we'll deal with them later, Camilla, it's a pity to waste time while Edie's here.' Edie beamed on him. Even Grandmother didn't pick Edie up as she so often did.

Edie was just going, an hour later when she said, 'By the way, when I joined the bus at Whangarei, who should I sit next to but Dilys Cranbourne's mother! Haven't seen her for weeks. Last time I saw her she was bubbling about Dilys's chances of marrying really well over there, someone owning a large estate in Hampshire. That sounded like her. She'd be one to marry where money was, if not *for* money. Given the chance, that is. But I think it must have fallen through. She's coming home before long—pity.'

Camilla looked sharply at her. 'Why pity? It would

be nice for her mother, wouldn't it?'

Edie always evaded clarification of her odd remarks. She looked vaguely about her. 'Where are my pearls?'

Jonathan said, 'I put them in the office, Edie. Camilla was always good at threading pearls. It's tricky if you aren't used to it—so she might as well do them. She's got some amber ones that need threading for re-sale. She bought them in a box of junk I've just gone through. Well, it's been lovely seeing you. My grandmother sent you her regards, by the way.'

Edie nodded, then surprisingly reverted to her previous topic. 'I meant pity she's coming now when you've just got back, Jonathan. She always had a soft spot for you, you know. Watch out she doesn't spoil things for you. Goodnight, all,' and off she went, bangles jingling, scarf-ends flying out as she stepped on to the verandah.

Elinor put aside her tatting and said, 'No wonder I put up with Edie! Once in a while she puts her finger on the right spot. Underneath all her silliness, she's pretty shrewd.'

Camilla sought for something to say, and came up with, 'Not to worry. Jonathan's shrewd too.'

He said slowly, 'Am I? Perhaps others do see us differently from the way we see ourselves. All I know about myself is that I'm ... vulnerable.'

Camilla walked out of the room. She didn't think he was. She thought he was tough. And he was playing on her emotions.

She was surprised how much her mind turned to the thought that Dilys was coming home. She found herself hoping it was just for a visit, and a short one at that. Why? What could it possibly matter to her? She found herself getting attached to the children. They were such fun, and Jonathan was so blessedly ordinary when they were around. What a pity their visit was to be so short ... There came the day when Jonathan looked up at the sky where a Boeing jet plane was zooming south down

Northland, looked at his watch and said, 'Prue and Wally's plane, for sure.'

Camilla shaded her eyes, looked up at it and said, 'That'll mean you'll be taking the children home soon.'

He said smoothly, 'Not too soon. I'll give Prue and Wally a day or two to settle down first. Why? Want to get rid of me?'

She frowned. 'You make everything too personal, Jonathan. Whether you're here of not, life for me goes on in the same old way, as you can see. The way I like it.'

It was untrue, but she wanted him to think that way. She was aware of his presence from breaking day till dewy eve and he somehow pursued her even into her sleep. It made her cross to dream about him all the time.

Jonathan laughed in a tantalising fashion. 'The word "like" is a very insipid word. You used to absolutely love life, Camilla. You bubbled over with sheer joy most of the time. That's a very placid, dull sort of relationship you've got with Greg. No fireworks.'

She felt her hands clench, then relaxed them lest he notice.

'Could be we save the fireworks for when you aren't about.'

'*Could* be, but I'll go bail you don't. You're the very last person I'd expect to drift into an attachment like that, tepid, comfortable and . . .'

'And what?'

'And second-rate.'

There was a touch of fire now in the look she turned on him. 'That's an extremely arrogant remark . . . you mean that having once been engaged to you, anyone else must be second-best?'

He ought to have looked angry, but instead he chuckled. 'I bet you never fly off at Greg like that! Which is what I mean. It must be tame. You and I, now, would have clashed gloriously at times . . . when we weren't just as ardently loving each other, rejoicing in being together. Even your voice is prosaic when you're talking to him on the phone.'

She said, 'Jonathan, there are times when I could take great pleasure in smacking your face . . . hard!'

Another chuckle. 'Again, that's what I mean. I bet you'd never be moved to smack Greg's. You'd pat it gently.'

Suddenly the anger left her. She said quietly and convincingly, 'Jonathan, don't sneer at Greg. Greg has come through a lot. And he and I understand each other. I'll never hurt him.'

For once she thought Jonathan seemed unsure of himself. The first time she had ever thought he might be, as he'd said, vulnerable. The slightest shade of alarm crossed his face. He said slowly, 'That's the first time I've seen you betray any sort of feeling about him. What has he come through, Camilla?'

She didn't set him back, she looked at him more candidly than she usually did, said, 'I could easily snap by saying it's none of your business, but that would be mean. Instead I'll just say that it's entirely confidential. Greg took a rap over something—the less said about it the better for everyone. I like and respect him.'

Jonathan's dark lean face looked reflective. 'H'm. But liking and respect aren't enough for a vital creature like you, Camilla. Don't make a mistake. You were always one for helping lame dogs over stiles. Don't confuse pity and concern, for the sort of feeling there ought to be in a marriage. That way shipwreck lies.'

She said slowly, 'Jonathan, you'd better understand that not only am I necessary to Greg, but Greg is also necessary to me. Please, don't spoil things.'

The plane had gone out of sight. Camilla was standing now with her hands on the pickets of the gate. Lavender rose from one side of it, balsam from the other. She pulled a red blossom of the balsam and a pungent green leaf, crushed them between her fingers, lifted them to her nose, then let the fragments fall. Just across the white dusty road the waters of the inlet, gentle here, lapped against the stone wall. The white masts of the smaller shipping gleamed against the sun, and the same sun struck a million facets from the wind-rippled surface of the water.

Over to the right, tourists were entering and leaving the old Trading Post, a stone building that had stood four-square to the elements since the first well-equipped missionary group had come here, pastors, teachers, carpenters, storekeepers, tillers of the ground.

Jonathan said, 'Our afternoon stint showing tourists through Hallows House is nearly upon us. Before they arrive, tell me you'll come down to Auckland with me when I return Victoria and Peregrine to Kohimarama Bay.'

Something in Camilla shrank from meeting Prue, to whom she'd be the girl who had jilted her brother. She said crisply, 'No, I won't, thanks.'

He protested, 'How mean! It's very awkward for a chap getting his niece to the Ladies.'

'Don't be ridiculous, you managed on the way up.'

'Yes, but only just at times. There's not always a convenient bush. You're a poor sport.'

She said candidly, 'Jonathan, I don't want to get involved with the whole family. Here, I can't help you being involved with mine, but that was none of my seeking. You and Grandmother did it deliberately. But please don't make it too tough for me. Besides, the Trading Post Ball is coming up next week, and I can't let Greg down for a partner.'

He looked at her with mock indignation, his dark heavy brows arched high. 'You don't care that I, the lonely stranger in your midst, will lack a partner?'

She said drily, 'A solitary male is always welcome at a dance, Jonathan. You could be a godsend.' She added impishly, 'Or you could escort Edie. Her husband hates dancing, won't be dragged there . . . and Edie can dance any one of us off our feet.'

Jonathan scowled. 'I'll get my own partner, thanks. She'd probably scatter beads all over the dance floor, or strangle me with one of her scarves. Talk about the dance of the Seven Veils ... she must own dozens! She even had one tucked into a bracelet the other night. Though there's something I can't help liking about her. She may drop bricks all over the place, but at least she recognises the reality of things, which is more than you do ... or more than you'll admit.'

Camilla was saved from answering because the tide of tourists pouring from a bus that had just swept down the hill and along the riverside road reached them. She unlatched the picket gate, said, 'Come right in. We've just opened,' and led the way up the shell path. 'Perhaps you'd like to see the garden first.'

By the time they reached the open door off the verandah, they were already enchanted. It had rained in the forenoon and every leaf had a raindrop pearled on it. Honeysuckle smothered old fences, periwinkle starred the grasses with blue, jasmine flung an exotic scent on the air, early roses, sweet and wholesome, counteracted its headiness, shasta daisies and forget-me-nots ran riot, a huge magnolia opened creamy chalices to the sun. Box hedges, six inches high, kept the crushed shells out of the flowerbeds, geraniums, wallflowers, cornflowers and larkspur fought for supremacy in a prodigality of leaf and bloom; wisteria hung in purple plumes along the old grey verandah posts.

They glimpsed the side garden, exclaiming delightedly over the millstones set as a path across the lawn to the brook that joined the river lower down, purple alyssum springing out of the centres of each, admired the bantams and Black Orpington hens and roosters picking contentedly about, and the snowy, stately geese.

'It's like something out of a Hans Andersen fairytale,' said someone. 'I could imagine a goosegirl taking her flock to pasture up a European hillside.'

Jonathan turned to the speaker and said, 'That's just what I saw the other morning. I heard a bit of a disturbance among the poultry before I was up. I stuck my head out of the window and saw Camilla here, in a blue-and-white gingham skirt, running barefoot in the dew, with the geese trailing after her. Quite idyllic, I assure you.'

They warmed to him. Here was a modern young man who was also a romantic. Almost instinctively they turned to him as the head of this household. He put a hand under Camilla's elbow as, ruffled with his calm assumption of the role, she went to leave them. He drew her with him as he ushered them into the parlour.

It was fascinating. The old piano with the candle-brackets, the music of a bygone taste in the songs open on the stand, the kerosene lamp on a bright circle of French knitting, laboriously done by some child, on a cotton reel and tacks; a cane rocker, a plush-covered one, old leather-bound books, an antimacassar in crochet done with the initials of Camilla's great-grandmother, who had also been Camilla. A round tapestry footstool, scrapbooks made by little fingers long since stilled, all these made for magic.

There was a Noah's ark on the shabby carpet, with chipped animals tumbling out of it, painted wooden engines and carriages, tiny bricks and red-coated metal soldiers lying scattered, as if any moment little boys in sailor suits and little girls in embroidered pinafores might rush in and start playing with them, quarrelling over them.

Jonathan was in fine fettle. He sat himself down at the piano, swept his fingers along the keys, his eyes on the open music, and sang in a very fine baritone, without a trace of embarrassment, 'O, believe me if all those endearing young charms, that I gaze on so fondly today . . .' and an inviting gesture had most of them joining in, 'Thou wouldst still be adored as this moment thou art, let thy loveliness fade as it will . . .' Very potent stuff, and the beggar knew it. They all fell for him.

A dear soul, probably in her nineties, said audibly as they finished, 'We're getting our money's worth today, for sure. I didn't think they made young men like that any more.'

He had absorbed the history of the place very well when he had listened to Camilla and Elinor conducting other parties round, so told them how the timber, the window mullions, the bricks and shingles had all been prepared on the site, that only the glass and the nails, the locks and the hinges had been imported.

'Some of the crochet work was done by Maori girls, who picked it up incredibly swiftly from Camilla's great-great-great-grandmother, Constancia Hallows. We're still using the same patterns, and Elinor, Camilla's grandmother, spends many evenings making them. There are some for sale in the showroom—pricey, but not over-priced for handmade stuff.'

There were delicate watercolours on the bedroom walls, mute testimony to the skills of former days, some incredibly good sketches the granddaughters of old Joshua had done under the expert eye of a governess in that schoolroom upstairs, signed Adeline, Emma, and Lorinda Hallows.

Jonathan said, 'A group like this is our favourite age-group. You are the ones who can remember the things your grannies used to treasure . . . the honeycomb quilts with the fringes, the music-boxes, the plush and silver photo-frames, the hairpin work of the tea-cloths, the wash-stands, the slates and slate-pencils, the willow-pattern tea-cups, the pot-pourri, the herb-bags, the sturdy Colonial furniture.'

'You've revived many memories very vividly for us,' said a merry-faced woman in her sixties. 'It's good to hold hands with the past. What I like about Hallows House is that it's still in the hands of the same family. I hope it always will be.'

At that moment Peregrine and Victoria burst in, each

with a bucket of shells. Peregrine forgot his manners, broke in with: 'Look ... Granny's going to show us how to make those shell-boxes like they did in the olden days. I'll keep things in mine.'

Victoria said: 'And *my* shells are going to make a nornament for my next birthday cake. A ballet dancer stepping out of an open shell ... Look, you use one of these fan shells——' she began rummaging in the bucket—'and you stand another one behind it and stick wee tiny shells made into flowers all round the edges ... where's that shell? Oh, at the bottom,' and she tipped the entire lot out, sand and all, on the old kauri floor.

The woman who'd hoped Hallows House would always be in the family said, turning to Camilla, 'How lovely! It looks as if the next generation's going to have the same interests. I suppose your children have it born and bred in them. And *isn't* your little boy like his father!'

There was a brief silence. Jonathan took a swift look at Camilla. She interpreted it correctly. He didn't want to squash these romantic notions, but Peregrine, blithely unaware, said firmly, 'Oh, *he's* not my father. He's my uncle, and this isn't our mum. They're not even married.'

Victoria looked up, a shell in each hand, 'But Mum says it's a pound to a penny they'll be married before next year's over. What *is* a pound? I know what a penny is.'

Camilla was grateful for the tagged-on question. She said hurriedly, 'That was the money we used to use in New Zealand way back in 1967—and in England they still use it. Though you'd be too young to remember. They're like our two-dollar notes. Jonathan, while you show them the baby's room with the wooden cradle, and the attic, I'll go over to the showroom to see if Wilma needs any help. By the way,' she turned to the group, 'you're very welcome to browse among the antiques there. No obligation to buy.' As she left, she couldn't help but notice that the women were smiling at each other knowingly as they followed Jonathan. She stayed behind long enough to pile Victoria's shells back in the bucket and sweep the sand up.

Well, at least she knew what Prue thought of the situation. Certainly she *wouldn't* go down to Kohimarama Bay with Jonathan. There were more than enough matchmakers here without having to fend off more in Auckland.

Jonathan rang Prue late that night. He used the living-room phone. They chatted on about the usual things; he assured her that not only had the children behaved like angels, but Elinor and Camilla had just loved having them. In fact, they were decided acquisitions to the continuing family saga when showing tourists round the older half of Hallows House! 'What do I mean?' they heard him say. Grandmother paused in her crocheting, listening for the answer. He chuckled, and winked at Camilla, who didn't avert her gaze quickly enough. 'Oh, a party of charming getting-on-a-bit tourists took them for Camilla's and mine, and were enchanted to think another generation kept up the family traditions. Like making shell-boxes, for instance. They're really much more like us than like either you or Wally. Beats me how two ginger-tops like you two produced Perry and Victoria.'

The pause probably indicated that Prue was giving him a bit of sisterly ear-bashing. He laughed, said, 'I say, the children don't even want to come home yet . . . I know Wally doesn't start till Monday. You've never seen Bay of Islands yet, and it's a dream. Why don't you set off tomorrow in the car? It's only about four hours. You'll just love Elinor . . . and Camilla.' At that moment he encountered a fierce glare from the latter. He grinned unrepentantly, then said suavely into the phone, but meant for Camilla's information, 'Of course it's all right: I'm not doing this off my own bat, chump.

Hallie suggested it earlier today when I told her Camilla couldn't come down with me. Just a moment, I'll put her on. Hallie, here you are.'

He dropped on to the couch facing the phone, beside Camilla, said, 'Now, no temper! You don't want to disappoint Greg over the Ball, so what was a chap to do? Oh, I meant to tell Prue it was on. She'd love that kind of dance, she's very fond of old-time dancing.' He dashed up, scribbled a memo, passed it to Elinor and returned to the couch.

Camilla said between her teeth, in a hissing whisper, 'I never knew anyone so determined to get his own way!'

Jonathan shrugged. 'An antidote to the frustration of the last five years. Don't begrudge me that. You really put me through the hoops.'

She ignored the last sentence and seized on the other. 'Yes. I realise that your ambitions were frustrated. Still, you've cancelled that out, haven't you? Instead of marrying into the business, you've now bought yourself in.'

She didn't think she had ever seen Jonathan colour up before, or seen such anger leap into his eyes either. In spite of speaking coolly and without fear, instinctively she drew back from him. But before he could get a word out, Hallie, turning from the wall instrument, said, holding out the phone, 'Jonathan, your sister wants to speak to you again.'

Camilla felt that his wrath would fall upon her the moment the receiver was replaced. Would it be any use pleading a headache and going up to her room? But he was angry enough to storm into her room and ask what the devil she meant by such an accusation. So it was with great relief that she heard at the best possible moment, while he was still talking to Prue, a step on the verandah, and the next moment Greg Peterson's big form filled the twilit gap between the room and the sky over the inlet beyond.

She got up quickly and went across to Greg, lifting

her face towards him. There was only a fragmentary hesitation till Greg kissed her full on the lips, just as Jonathan replaced the receiver and swung round.

Perhaps only Camilla saw the tightness of his mouth. His voice was casual. 'Oh, hullo, Peterson, the very man I wanted to see. I was just speaking to my sister. They got back from Raratonga today, and Hallie's kindly invited them up till Sunday, to spend the balance of their holiday, and pick up the youngsters. I saw Edward earlier and he's going to take us out in one of the smaller launches, and he mentioned that your people have retired on their holiday island . . . said if I got in touch with you, you might be able to say if they'd mind if we had a shore picnic there. Edward said it's so safe for children for swimming. What do you think?'

Greg said, 'I'm sure it would be fine by them. There's a barbecue down by the rocks, and there's a sort of natural paddling-pool in the rocks after the tide goes down. I'm going there with some provisions tomorrow—in fact I came in to see if Camilla might go with me. I'll ask them then. How about it, Camilla? Just in the morning.'

Camilla looked delighted. That would get her away from Jonathan for a few hours at least. 'It would be wonderful! What a blessing Jonathan's here. He's proving such a success with the tourist parties, especially the older ones, playing them the ditties of a century ago, no less, that they'd sooner have him than me, I know. Well, that's all settled . . . Greg, I'll walk down to the shore with you . . . I suppose you parked down there?'

'Yes, but don't I get my usual coffee?'

Camilla said firmly, 'You do, but in the tea-garden of the Trading-Post. They've decided to stay open an hour or two in the evenings from now on.'

She tucked her hand in his arm, went out of the door with him, turned and said, 'See you tomorrow morning, folks,' and went out, the very symbol of a girl eager to spend the gloaming with the loved one.

Greg demanded as they closed the picket behind them and went across the road to the jetty, looking down into the sheeny green waters, 'And what was all that about?'

There was a break in Camilla's voice which made him look at her sharply. 'I goofed—I goofed badly. I said something very nasty to Jonathan. Oh, it was something true, that I know, but he was furious. He was about to have a bit of me when you walked in. I reckon he was going to bawl me out in front of Grandmother.'

Greg put his arm about her, gave her a comforting hug, turned her round to face him. They weren't to know that Jonathan was staring out moodily at the tide, and could see them plainly through the gap in the lilacs.

Greg said quietly, 'It doesn't pay, does it, Camilla? You're only hurting yourself. Take it easy, pal. I don't really know what it's about except that for once I seem to have served you instead of you serving me. And I'll keep on doing it as long as it doesn't fog things up between you and Jonathan.'

A spark of resentment came into the brown eyes that were bright with tears. '*Fog* them up? Things between Jonathan and me were *blotted out* completely, long ago. It's only that it makes me so furious to be thrust into such close quarters with him. It's not fair. I'd like to get out of it.'

'But you can't, because of your grandmother. Don't do anything rash, Camilla. Time will take care of it.'

She said passionately, 'I *hate* time. It cheats us, robs us of all the joy we ought to have in these years. You most of all, Greg.'

His face was very grave. 'I know, Camilla. But I've learned to live with it. And perhaps worst of all for me is that I know I'm helpless to ease Meg's burden.' For a moment a faint smile softened his face. 'But she's magnificent, no other word for it. My sister tells me. Of course her nursing training stood her in good stead. And he's been marvellous, too—so patient. If anyone deserves to win back to full health he does. I'm so glad he never knew how near it had come to a parting of the ways for him and Meg. What would he have had left to live for? The rest of his family wiped out and himself reduced to a wheelchair.'

Camilla felt choked with the pity she knew for all of them. She couldn't express it in words. She stood on tiptoe and put her face against his, put her arms about him—the age-old gesture of sympathy. Nothing more. Those two knew that, but to the spectator it spoke volumes. Jonathan shut the French windows very quietly.

Camilla found her voice, said, 'You've one thing left, Greg. You've got all your dreams and ideals intact. *Meg* didn't have feet of clay.'

Greg looked at her sharply. 'Camilla, you've helped me and Meg tremendously, from that first tricky moment when we thought Morris might have suspected. But you've never said much about your broken romance. Why you ended it, for instance. I've never wanted to pry. I met Jonathan only once five years ago, and that so briefly, but since meeting him again, I like him very much. But now you say Meg didn't have feet of clay—as if Jonathan had. I can't believe it . . . yet if it made you break your engagement, it must have been something serious. Want to tell, or not? But whether you do or don't, if it was someone making mischief, make sure it's true. Because he strikes me as a very upright sort of chap.'

They walked across to the tea-rooms, sat out at a table under a walnut just coming into full leaf, had coffee, fragrant and steaming hot, brought to them, and slices of apple sponge in which Camilla wasn't interested at all.

She said slowly, 'I'd rather not talk about it, Greg. It's not a problem to be solved. Nobody made mischief, and what happened was only too true. I asked about it, when I found out, and was given a truthful answer. In fairness to Jonathan I ought to say it wasn't a case of unfaithfulness ... he wasn't playing about with anyone else. Only what happened destroyed my trust in him. He doesn't know I know about it. I didn't want to ally my life with his any more, or have him linked with Hallows House in any way. But now he's here. He couldn't marry into the firm, so he's bought his way in. Secretly, too, in collusion with my grandmother—took advantage of her age, I suppose, when she was in London.'

Greg said slowly, 'You seem very sure. Yet I could swear that he seems——'

She interrupted him and there was bitterness in her tone. 'Yes, I know! He seems genuinely fond of me. He's arrogant with it, cocksure, he even deceives himself. I think he's persuaded himself that his is the love of a lifetime. I imagine very few people ever admit, even to themselves, that although they wouldn't exactly marry for money, they would marry where money is. Not that Grandmother is exactly wealthy, and we'll all share in it, Rose, and her three children, Uncle Edward too, because Gran loves him like a son, but it's a case of business opportunity. And I can't go away because I want, above all else, to see that Hallows House remains the byword it has always been in the antique business ... for absolute integrity.'

Greg reached across the table, took her hand, gripped it as a brother might have done and said, 'I know you said you hated time, but in this case, it could be your ally. Your judgment five years ago was only that of a girl of twenty, not an experienced judgment. Sometimes the years passing make us more tolerant. I don't mean a lowering of standards, but an understanding of what has made people we love, act as they did *in the past*. Finish your apple cake, and let's go for a walk up the hill. I'll keep you out late enough so that you don't have to face Jonathan's wrath when you get back. By morning you'll be less tense and he may have simmered down.'

So she came home to a house in darkness. Even Jonathan's light was out, and normally he read far into the night. She had the horrible feeling that for once in her lifetime Hallows House was hostile to her. Oh, how she wished Jonathan Lemaire had stayed thirteen thousand miles away!

CHAPTER FIVE

To Camilla it seemed an insult that the day should be so supremely beautiful when she felt so miserable. She'd tossed and turned all night, going over what she'd said to Jonathan. How he'd looked. Oh, how stupid to care so deeply when she knew so well that money mattered most to him. That it mattered so much he'd diddled an old lady out of a large sum of money, broken the law in smuggling it out of New Zealand without notification. The fact that she felt so guilty for having said what she had, made her more furious than ever. It was surely a case of the cap fitting and so Jonathan wearing it. But why *had* he looked like that?

Well, she worked it out, somewhere about three in the morning, the most hopeless time of all to those who cannot sleep because conscience or despair or grief is gnawing at them. No one liks to admit, even to one's inner self, that one's motives are less than honourable. If Jonathan had been one of the ones—and still was— who would marry where money was, he'd probably never have owned it to himself. He had probably kidded himself that he truly loved this girl who would inherit the antique business and Hallows House. After all, she was quite personable, so it wouldn't exactly have been a sacrifice, and there was no doubt but what his grand-mother would have brought her own wishful thinking to bear upon the young Jonathan. What could be more idyllic than the children of two bosom friends marrying?

Most men, receiving the sort of letter Camilla had sent him when she broke the engagement, telling him in a skilfully written way that once he'd gone back to England, she had realised it wasn't love with her, only infatuation, would have accepted that.

In fact, she had thought he had, after his abortive attempt at reconciliation had failed, and she had gone to Australia to escape him. So it meant that suddenly it had flared up again. *What* had flared up? she asked herself, turning her pillow over again. Not the sudden realisation that he still loved her, but two or three factors ... his own desire to be free of his older brothers' domination in the business, his love of New Zealand, and Gran's visit to London, with a cunning proposition.

He had hoped that her own still unattached state, plus the fact that in time to come, with her grandmother approaching a great age, she would need more family support in the business than Uncle Edward's family could spare from their own big-game fishing fleet ... and perhaps the memory of how, five years ago, she had certainly responded ardently to him ... that all these things would add up to a resumption of their engagement, with, no doubt, a marriage to follow soon. At the memory of how she had loved him, how eager the young Camilla had been to be married as soon as the tide of tourists ebbed, in the March, and to fly off with Jonathan to an English summer, she burned with humiliation.

She reached up and turned her light on. She had shut her door, so no one should see and guess. So that Gran wouldn't come padding in, all solicitude because she was having a wakeful night, and ask questions. So that Jonathan wouldn't guess she even cared she had upset him. *He* was the one who ought to be having a wakeful night, knowing she'd seen through him all that time ago.

She tried to read two magazines, but put them down after several attempts. It was so easy to solve a love-problem on paper. Or was it? Hadn't she read once that authors often found their characters taking over, getting out of step? Oh, what did it matter? Stories were out. She padded over to her bookcase. There was that volume of poetry Edie had given her only last week. Poor silly Edie, who thought Jonathan the epitome of any girl's dream. She hadn't read it yet—mainly because she'd been cross with the way Edie had looked at the two of them, said inane things, had encouraged Jonathan in his maddening assumption that things were working out very well, that everything in the garden was lovely.

Camilla's mouth felt dry. She picked up the glass of water by her bed. Ugh! It was such a sultry night for October ... perhaps a very hot summer was on its way. Tepid water was ghastly. But she wasn't going down to the fridge for a cold drink. She wanted no encounters.

She got back into bed with a book of poetry. She'd read till her lids got so drowsy they wouldn't stay open.

It was surprisingly good. A collection of New Zealand and Australian verse taken from a magazine very popular years ago. These poets had really spent time on their verse construction ... days and days, probably, singing the words over in their minds. Some were quite simple, full of quiet joys in stay-at-home days.

Her eyes blurred. That was all she'd ever wanted—a home with Jonathan, Oh, this book too was full of happy ending stuff. Hadn't any of these writers ever suffered?

She turned a page. Ah, this was more in keeping with her mood.

> 'The sea has known the fury of the storm,
>   The demons of unrest have ridden high
> Upon each wave, towards each mighty cliff
>   And shrieked with hatred from the riven sky!
> But now it lies a placid bay of blue,
>   Its passion spent beneath the tempest's will,
> Serene and calm since at the break of day
>   It's Maker whispered softly, "Peace, be still."

'I too have known the fury of the storm,
A tumult of unrest within my heart,
But now, spent with emotions I am still
And rest untroubled in a world apart.
God, send the little winds, the burning sun,
The magic of the moon, the beating rain,
To stir the tides of love within my breast
So I may live and laugh and weep again!'

Yet at the moment she didn't want to laugh and weep again. She would rather be in that unemotional state of not feeling anything. Of not longing for the days when she had loved Jonathan and believed in him, of not finding bitter things rising on her lips, of subduing some, not managing to subdue others, and then knowing regret, as now, regret that was keeping her from the healing hours of sleep. It was ridiculous, knowing what she knew about him, that all she could think of was that hurt, vulnerable look on his face last night, superseded a moment later by fury. Oh, would morning never come?

Well, now it had, and thank heaven she wasn't spending it here ... Greg would take her out in that silver-hulled boat of his, beyond the Gate of Heaven, to the shining beauty of the larger Bay of Islands, to the kindliness and tranquillity of Greg's parents' holiday home, away from Jonathan, from tourists, from the sentimental atmosphere of Hallows House that stifled her so much.

She pulled back her curtains ... usually she didn't sleep with them drawn, but the young moon had made her room too light, and had helped keep her from sleep.

How stupid to resent the loveliness of the new day, when, had it been raining, or the bay wind-tossed into a seething cauldron of angry waves, Greg might have decided to postpone his trip. But somehow this superlative beauty seemed to deride her ... to mock her misery.

The bell-birds were chiming as if this were the loveliest

day of all the year, honeysuckle and wallflowers were vying with each other to scent the dewy morning; the larks, out of sight, were adding their own exquisite music to the songs of the mating thrushes; the brook was singing happily over its mossy stones on its way to the river and thence to the sea ... even one of the bantams felt the impulse to be loved and spread an inviting wing before the lord and master of the bantam kingdom. An idyll, yes ... but you had to be in the mood for it.

Camilla made her bed, picked up the inoffensive book of poetry, better get that sentimental volume back in her bookcase. She didn't want Gran to see what she'd been reading. She dropped the book putting it in, and it fell open at a page she hadn't read. She glanced at it because at the foot was a comment, scrawled in ballpoint. It just said, 'How true!' Edie's writing. A faint interest stirred Camilla. She read:

'Grief swept my heart ... God's lovely world
Seemed steeped in gloom ... each raindrop pearled
On leaf and blade seemed wept for me,
Gone moonlight's charm, Spring's witchery;
And when the stars forbore to shine
Night's sombre mood seemed part of mine,
What arrogance to thus believe
That all the world with me must grieve!

'But oh! It seemed so right and fair
When joy succeeded dire despair,
That I should find in every tree
An echo of my ecstasy!
Sure ... every bird burst forth in praise
For dreamless nights and carefree days,
And in Earth's budding-forth I found
My happiness with Springtime crowned!'

Camilla's eyes fell on Edie's scribbled comment again. 'How true!' she had written. Edie, of course, was a rattle-pate. But who knew what storms in life she had weathered? She was fun, and kind, and Gran said she so often hit the nail on the head.

Suddenly, impatiently, she slammed the book shut and returned it to the shelf. The day was here, however beautiful it might be, and there were certain preliminaries she must get through before Greg came. She couldn't skip assisting with the children's breakfast, or taking her grandmother's in. But somehow she'd dodge eating with Jonathan and Victoria and Peregrine.

She breezed into the kitchen airily, a would-be gay good-morning on her lips. But the kitchen was empty. The middle table-mat was there, bearing the milk, butter, sugar, cornflakes and raisins, and a dish of bananas. On the sink bench was her grandmother's tray all set out, and a pile of used dishes. A note stood under the toast-rack. She plucked it from under. It said:

'Promised the children I'd take them at low tide to the Little Cove, for some tiny shells they want for their boxes. Have a good day. J.'

Camilla ought to have felt relief, but instead she felt as if he'd slapped her face. She tightened her lips, made herself one piece of toast, dropped a tea-bag in a cup. Then she prepared the dainty breakfast her grandmother loved, fresh grapefruit juice from their own trees, triangles of toast, tangelo marmalade, tea in a flowered pot. Jonathan had begun putting a flower on Hallie's tray every morning. He hadn't omitted it. There was a tiny sweetheart-rose and two cornflowers, held together by a scrap of raffia.

She thought her grandmother was studying her rather closely. She managed to avoid comment, though— talked lightheartedly about how glorious it was to have a day off. 'I'm beginning to think you did me a great service in bringing in a partner.' Gran gave no sign of feeling curious or disturbed, but as Camilla left the room she said, 'Give my love to Mr and Mrs Peterson,' then added, 'By the way, has Greg heard recently how Morris is?'

She answered from outside in the hall. 'He heard from Meg's sister that he's a little improved—signs of movement in his toes. I asked Greg last night. Gran, I'm going to slip over to the Trading Post to get a large tin of mixed biscuits for Greg's mother. She gets such a lot of company, and half the folk who drop in forget she's supposed to be on holiday and not there to just provide for their appetites.'

'Very proper. You can take one of the fruit cakes out of our freezer if you like, it's a good standby.'

Camilla called back her thanks, and went back to the kitchen. She washed up before she slipped across the road to the Trading Post. She was extremely glad that Greg's Silver Lady came round the south headland of the bay before there was any sign of Jonathan and his niece and nephew returning. It could be that the ensuing hours before they met again would abate his anger somewhat.

Greg and Camilla returned at sunset, coming home across a pewter sea reflecting the rose and amber of the western sky on the hills that climbed behind Hallows House and on the gleaming white walls and red roof of St James' Church that old Joshua Hallows had built to the glory of God in the long ago. As they came up from the jetty, they looked the perfect picture of holiday happiness, Greg wearing a peaked cap and sky-blue shorts and shirt, Camilla in white shorts and a sun-top piped with blue, her skin apricot-tan against it, blue sandals on her feet; her hair, bleached lighter by the long day in the sun, flowing out freely, wind-tossed and curling at the ends. She carried a string of fish in one hand. The other was clasping Greg's lightly. They were singing a sea-shanty together as they came. Quite a good act. They'd planned it that way.

They padded across the verandah. Camilla waved her fish. 'We had a very successful day. Greg's got these all ready for the deep-freeze. And in that bag he's carrying are scallops and mussels Mrs Peterson sent you, Gran. They're already frozen—we wrapped them well. I'll just go through and put them in the freezer. Greg, I'll rustle you up a snack before you go.'

Hallie said smoothly, 'Sorry about that, Greg, but the Portmans in Puriri Cove are having a big barbecue party tonight, as you know, and your man rang up to say one of your boats has broken down, and he wants you to get back as soon as possible to pick up all they couldn't accommodate; I gather it's a twenty-first, so you wouldn't like to let them down, Paddy said.'

Camilla subdued her dismay. She'd wanted Greg to stay as long as possible. He grimaced, as if loth to leave her, then said, 'Well, needs must when the devil drives . . . come on down to the boat with me, Camilla. There's that other package to come up.'

Jonathan said, 'Is it heavy? Shall I come?'

Greg assured him, 'No, very light. Besides——' he grinned and might just as well have said: 'Don't be a spoilsport, I want to kiss my girl goodnight.'

Camilla thrust the string of fish and the shellfish at Jonathan. 'Put the wrapped stuff in the freezer, please, and leave the other on the kitchen bench, would you? I'll have to bag it.' She went out again with Greg. She even managed a chuckle as she said goodbye to him, without kissing, as this corner of the jetty couldn't be seen from the house.

'You've sure squared any debt you owe me, Greg. Thanks a lot. You've saved my pride.'

He turned back as he went to step aboard and cast off. 'Make sure it's worth it, that's all, Camilla. I've heard it said that pride is a cold bedfellow.'

She stood for some time gazing blankly after the wake of the vessel, as twilight fell.

She came in, said, 'I'm for a shower . . . don't think I'll bother with a snack for myself. We seem to have been eating all day.'

Her grandmother had disappeared. Jonathan said, 'Your shower can wait. I've got something to say to you.'

Her heart thudded against her ribs. She said quickly, 'What about the children? Isn't it time they went to bed?'

He said expressionlessly, 'Aunt Rose is doing that for us tonight. They've gone early because she promised them she'd read them four stories. Come on.'

She said nervously, and felt furious with herself for betraying her feelings, 'Come on where? Can't you say what you want to say here?'

'No, I can't. This is no place. I don't want the telephone to ring, or Edie drop in, or Sarah and Caroline. I don't want anyone within earshot when I bawl you out. We're going to the summerhouse.'

Camilla moistened her lips. 'Bawl me out? What can you mean? I'm not a child, to be summoned to the Head's study.'

She'd never seen Jonathan look like this before—lips in a straight line, his face so colourless he looked darker than ever, his eyes narrowed, his expression unreadable.

Neither had he ever spoken to her this way. 'Did you really think you could get away with saying a thing like that to me? Without being asked to explain it? Now if you want it in private, off to the summerhouse. If you want it in public, stay here, where some of the clan will probably pop in every five minutes. But whichever way it is, you're going to give me an explanation. And right away. No rushing off to try to calm yourself. No tidying-up. No putting warpaint on. Get going!'

Speechless, her heart racing, Camilla turned and walked out of the room, to the back field where the goat and the donkey grazed and where the old round summerhouse stood, its frail trellised sides held together by the vines and rambler roses of a century ago. Here Constancia Hallows used to wait for Joshua as he returned from his missionary journeys by boat in the

days when this was a wild untamed country, and Russell,
or Kororareka as it was called then, across the Bay, was
a hell-hole of the Pacific, with whalers and grog-shops
and the pitiful outcasts of other civilisations. Here
Adeline, Emma and Lorinda Hallows had entertained
their beaux in a Victorian age; here she and Jonathan,
long ago, had sat and kissed and dreamed up a whole
future together. He didn't care. This was the place he'd
chosen to bawl her out.

She went up the rickety old steps ahead of him, went
right into the centre of the floor, stood and faced him,
willing her hands not to tremble by clasping them together in front of her. A little cool wind sprang up, sweeping in from the sea and up the inlet. One moment her
skin had been burning with too much sun. Now it turned
to gooseflesh.

Tall as she was, she still had to look up at him and
she felt it put her at a disadvantage. For all her inward
fears, however, she looked as cool as a pond-lily, and
she lifted her chin.

'Yes, Jonathan,' she said. 'I'm waiting for the fireworks.'

'And you're going to get them. Of all the contemptible
things . . . to fire off an accusation like that at me when
Hallie was in the room and talking to my sister on toll!
Giving me no chance whatever to answer it, just leaving
me to seethe about it, and going off with Greg Peterson.
But you're going to answer for it now. This whole thing
is to do with money, isn't it?'

Her lips were a straight line too. 'Yes, it is. Always
has been.'

'*Always has been?* Don't be absurd! How *could* it be?
Five years ago it was just a love affair that went wrong.
We fell in love, planned marriage. I departed to find us
somewhere to live in London, meaning to return here
with you if you didn't like it. On my part it lasted . . .
the attachment. On yours it was just infatuation, or so
you said. Absence killed it stone dead.'

Her mind felt as if it was scurrying here and there, trying to find a means of excuse, of escape.

He continued: 'Now you say it's money, as if I were a fortune-hunter or something. You must be mad! I've tried to fathom it out, as it applies *now*, not *then*—that's beyond me. I think you must have worked it out that though by now you'd imagined my feeling for you was as dead as mutton, when Hallie came to London I saw in it a good chance to buy in, come out here, make up to you again, therefore get control of the business through marrying you, and feather my own nest. Am I right? Answer me . . . if you aren't too chicken!'

Camilla said, 'Yes, *you are right*. In fact, spot on.'

If possible his features grew even more forbidding. He said, 'You'll have to elaborate. A plain statement like that does nothing to explain *why* you thought that. Good heavens, this is a tinpot business compared with Lemaire's of London. *It's* known all over the world.'

She said in as level a tone as she could manage: 'You're a big family. Your grandparents both have shares. Your parents have, so do your brothers and their wives. My guess is that you don't like being the youngest. You want to spread yourself. And you could quite easily think there could be profitable sidelines here.'

This time his control slipped to show surprise and curiosity. 'What *can* you mean?'

Camilla wished she hadn't said that.

Jonathan said, implacably, 'I want a specific answer to that. What sideline, for instance?'

She moistened her lips. 'Well, sometimes our rarer treasures here fetch terrific prices overseas. You could be planning to go seeking out things you know would bring more——'

He had a flush on his cheeks now. 'It's quite incredible, but I think that you must be thinking of Maori artifacts. It must be because most of the other things available here are much more plentiful in the U.K., or all over Europe. I once heard of an instance of this, in the trade. But how dare you think that Lemaire's would ever be associated with such a thing! You must be out of your mind!'

In that instant, Camilla's heart hardened against him. That had been his chance. He could have confessed that once he had succumbed to temptation of that sort, but never again.

He made an impatient gesture. 'Anyway, forget that— it's too absurd for words. I think you ought to go right into the whole business deal with your grandmother. It cost me a good deal to buy into the business—I had to borrow from Grandfather. Certainly he wouldn't take interest on it, and some of it's part of my inheritance-to-be. Steve and Randall had some advanced when they got married. Mother and Dad put money into it too, even though it was tough on Mother, another of her brood coming to live thirteen thousand miles away. But of course you'd never have given a thought to that!

'But what's this business about *it always has been*? Was it not only that you didn't care enough for me, once I'd gone back home, five years ago? What did you suspect me of then?'

When Camilla didn't answer because she was seeking for the right words, he added, 'Just say what you really think. Don't haver about, trying to justify yourself. Last night you accused me of still wanting to marry into the business, talked of my frustrated ambitions. Now you say it's *always* been money. I'm waiting for you to explain that. You couldn't have believed, surely, that I was marrying you for money, for the business?'

She said, 'I came to believe just that—that ultimately money mattered most to you. Oh, I think you found me quite attractive, so perhaps you weren't marrying me solely for money, but certainly where money was. Then, even more than now, you were overshadowed by your much older brothers. It was an opportunity and you took it.'

His voice was low, intense, but it had exactly the same

effect as if he'd shouted at her. 'Any chance that you'll do the decent thing and tell me of any instances that made you think this of me?'

Her voice didn't shake; she was glad of that. She said, 'I don't think it's necessary for me to do that. Why should I pinpoint those things that led me to that conclusion? I came to realise that money was what mattered most to you in life. I felt it put both me and the business in jeopardy. Now it's only the business that's at risk. But I'm here to see that our dealings are carried through with the same sort of integrity that's characterised Hallows House since the time the first Joshua began his missionary journeys and opened up the Trading Post. There was never, in the whole of his long life, the slightest hint of any shady land deals with the Maoris as there was with others. He came to serve these people. When danger threatened as misunderstanding grew, the local Maoris protected him, loved him and Constancia and their children. Most of all they respected and trusted him. I'm the principal heir, as it happens, so I'm going to be very careful who I marry. Big business and big business methods have no place here in Reikorangi.'

Jonathan lost his cool for a moment, said violently, 'Meaning that the business methods Lemaire's of London employ are less honest than Hallows'? I resent that. Not just for myself, but for my grandfather and my great-grandfather. In fact right back to the days when my forebears fled from the French Revolution and in abject poverty began restoring old furniture. I won't have you sneering at business methods in London from this cramped and insular corner of the globe, you smug little devil!'

She flinched. She knew not what to say. In spite of what she knew about him, and her underlying fear of his anger, something deep within her admired the way he stood up for his grandfather, his ancestors.

She'd never seen Jonathan's mouth set in a sneer before. He said: 'You've got an absolute obsession about this, it seems.' He gave a short laugh of pure contempt that made her want to strike him. 'Heavens, what drama! You sound like Elizabeth the First determining to remain a Virgin and wed no man, because she didn't want to endanger England. Right! It's all over. I came back here because, fool that I was, I couldn't believe that we wouldn't grow together again. Because I always felt that our marriage had been meant to happen. I was very sure of myself, arrogant if you like. I wouldn't believe I couldn't win you all over again. But not now. *I don't want you.*

'The Camilla I loved was just a figment of my imagination. What a fool I was! *That* Camilla just doesn't exist, probably never did. You spoke to me of *my* ambitions. It occurs to me that *you're* stiff with ambition, chock-full. You wanted to run the whole thing yourself when you fell heir to it, didn't you? Well, I've thwarted you in that, all unknowing. My hands are tied, temporarily at least. My money is sunk in it.

'It cost a mighty lot to put it through. My parents and my grandparents were magnificent about it. They even thought it would give me a better chance with you ... winning you back ... if I owned shares. What a fiasco! But don't feel too badly, my would-be tycoon ... in years to come you just may find yourself the sole head of the business. I won't hurt Hallie. I won't put a rift between her and her lifetime friend, my grandmother. I'll wait till it can't hurt anyone else ... then I'll pull out and go back to England and start a new business entirely of my own. But it won't obsess me as yours does you. You'll realise your ambition, perhaps, and I'd be less than human if I didn't hope that you'll find ambition a cold bedfellow.'

It was such an echo of what Greg had said to her so short a time ago that an involuntary sound of pain escaped her. Jonathan looked at her curiously, but still with contempt in his eyes.

Camilla swallowed, ran her tongue over her dry lips

and said, 'What are we going to do? Now, I mean.'

He shrugged. 'What else but carry on putting on a show of being reasonably good friends? So that they all come to realise that it doesn't matter a fig to us, working together. So that they know old ashes can't be warmed up if the essential spark is missing. And I'll tell you this—I won't have my sister made unhappy over it. She, like all the rest of the matchmakers, will give up in time. She's always wanted to meet you. She's quite fond of her youngest brother, odd as it may seem to you. As soon as she came to New Zealand she wrote to ask why didn't I come out to them for a holiday, and made no secret of her reason.

'You'll behave with hospitality towards her. We've got to hide this from everyone, do you hear? I won't have you making anyone unhappy because of some stupid bee buzzing in your bonnet. It's all over. It's the way you want it and it's the way I want it now. That's all . . . you can go. I'll come in later. I'll go for a walk.'

Without another word she turned and stumbled from the summerhouse.

Jonathan had been quite wrong when he said it had to be hidden from everyone. Poor Uncle Edward, mending the roof of the ancient building, was sitting frozen on the ladder he'd hooked over the turreted edge where the angles of the sections met in the centre-point of the roof. They'd got into their furious argument so quickly, he hadn't had a chance to clamber down and give them warning that they had an eavesdropper. Then the ferocity of their quarrel had held him there in sheer embarrassment . . . terrified of being discovered.

He was cramped in his legs and arms, and horrified in his spirit. Who could have guessed at what lay behind that broken engagement? How could his adored niece think such a thing of Jonathan? There *must* be something behind it. Jonathan should have shaken it out of her. Well, with that between them, it wouldn't matter what the clan did, here or in England, there wasn't much hope of a reconciliation.

Five seconds later Uncle Edward was relieved to hear Jonathan stride out of the summerhouse. He crouched down as he realised from the footsteps that he was making for the back gate of the field, en route for the river path. Do him good to walk it off, poor Uncle Edward thought. He had no heart to finish his job. It would do tomorrow. And it would be ghastly if Jonathan came back to find him up here, and suspected their quarrel had been overheard. Very quietly he moved his cramped ankles and knees, worked his way down, left his gear up there but removed the ladder when he'd reached the ground.

He flexed his muscles, hoped no one in the house was looking out of a window, and disappeared between the orchard trees, making for a seldom-used path that would lead him to other stepping-stones over the brook to the sanctuary of his own place. He'd go down to their private boat-house and do a job or two there, to restore his shattered nerves and try to think of some way to help.

Half an hour later he came to the conclusion that no one could do a darned thing. It was all washed up. There was only one consolation: the fact that the two concerned were going to say nothing to any of the others. Outwardly they were to continue much as before. Had there been a definite rupture—had Jonathan pulled out and revealed here, and to his family in London, just what Camilla had believed of him, a coolness could have developed, if not full estrangement, between the two families.

Camilla called out to her grandmother from the foot of the stairs. 'Gran, I'm going to have a shower and wash the salt out of my hair. And I think I'll turn in early tonight. Sun and sea always make me sleepy.'

'Right. I'm going to be early tonight myself. Where's Jonathan?'

'Gone for a walk. I'm too tired after all that swimming. I'll look in on the children before I go to sleep. Night-night.'

Old Elinor smiled to herself. She knew very well Jonathan had hated Camilla going off for the day with Greg. Not that he need fear; they were no more than good friends. But Camilla, she suspected, didn't want to drop like a ripe plum into Jonathan's lap, not when she'd been the one to sever their engagement. But Elinor was certain that for her wilful granddaughter there had never been anyone else to accelerate her pulse, and, all unknowing, she went happily off to bed. And to sleep. Which was something not all the household achieved.

CHAPTER SIX

CAMILLA, against her will, loved Prudence Lane and Wally on sight. What a sister-in-law she would have made! She was so full of fun, so obviously in love with Wally, with her children, with life, and she had a close bond with her brother.

The ginger hair Jonathan had spoken of was a glorious auburn, and her eyes were like her brother's but not quite so dark. She had a faint powdering of freckles across her nose, and was one of the lucky redheads, the sun of Raratonga hadn't reddened it.

She seemed to dance through life. Camilla, who had moved in a trance since she and Jonathan had had their showdown, found herself responding in spite of her heavy heart. Even so it seemed incredible to her at times that the whole family didn't know that something had occurred. Yet their ignorance helped both of them to appear normal. At least she supposed it helped Jonathan too. Or perhaps his nonchalance was natural. Perhaps he just didn't care, now.

To the others it must have seemed as if he teased and fooled with Camilla as before, because constantly the quips and jests flew backwards and forwards. It was such a holiday atmosphere, swimming, boating, exploring the little village, with Prue and Wally revelling in the history. Only Camilla knew that Jonathan's eyes never sought hers in that exchange of looks that she'd been becoming used to again, that he didn't say the dear outrageous things that so amused her grandma, that he'd dropped his proprietorial airs that had so irritated her at first, that when their eyes did meet, occasionally, the look in his was always shuttered.

Prue was walking with Camilla down the Colonial

Shopping Mall that had been built recently, complete with white iron lace and small-paned windows, bright with tropical flowers in painted tubs, as reminiscent of another age as could be. They were in search of candy mice for Peregrine and Victoria, consolation presents for the absence of the grown-ups at the Ball the next night, when Caroline and Sarah were to babysit with them.

'I just love Reikorangi,' said Prudence suddenly. 'It dreams. Dreams of its past, I suppose. It seems to me your ancestors founded it on happiness, on harmony. I know they faced great privations and dangers, and must have known terrible homesickness for all that was familiar and dear, but they seemed to bring their aura of happiness with them.

'You can sense it everywhere. In the bedroom upstairs, for instance. Oh, I suppose it's foolish and romantic of me, but I have a feeling it's never known a really unhappy marital hour. Wally said so last night, as we lay there watching the moon through the window, just before we drifted off to sleep. He just said quietly, "Don't you think this has always been a happy bedroom, Prue? Tranquil?" I was so lucky to get Wally,' she mused. 'He's articulate, shares his thoughts with me. So I told him I'd been imagining the same, that despite all you hear about Victorian prudery and suppressed feelings, I felt that in this room there'd always been a glad response and understanding. I've never believed all Victorian wives were frigid. Oh, listen to me! Wally teases sometimes and says it's because I was brought up in an antique atmosphere. But I loved it all so much, the stories behind the pieces Lemaire's were selling—or, in some instances, keeping. Camilla, can we go behind the shops and join up with the lane to Hallows Green? We can? Then come on!'

The lane was full of fragrance and birdsong, English trees lived in glad harmony with *rimu* and *kahikitea* and *kowhai*. Lantanas in golds and scarlets, mauves and pale yellows filled the spaces between the trees with symmetrical circles of beauty; tall foxgloves swayed in the slight breeze, thousands of ferns sprang from every crevice of the native trees.

Prudence continued her theme. 'We're all like that, specially Jonathan. He's such a softy. Stephen and Randall thought when he first started with the firm that the business would never show a profit if they let him out round the villages hunting stock. He's been known to advise people to hang on to antiques, that they appreciate. But Grandpa said to let him go, that profit wasn't everything. What did you say, Camilla?'

Her throat was suddenly dry. 'I didn't say anything, I—I just coughed.' It had stabbed her, Prue's trust in her brother. It was so misplaced. She must change the subject. 'Did you and Jonathan decide on what he's to sing at the Ball? I left you to it, but it sounded as if you really disagreed later. Who won?'

'Jonathan, of course,' said Prue gloomily. 'He was right, I had no business to ask him to sing that. He said they wanted the gay old-timers, not the sadder ones. Only I couldn't resist trying. I wanted——'

'Go on. What did you want?'

Prue hesitated, then plunged. 'I'd like you to have heard him sing *Aftermath*. Do you know it? I brought a copy up with me—hunted all over Auckland for it. He refused point-blank, and no wonder. He knew exactly what I was up to.'

'You mean he sings it well? It suits his voice? But——'

'I mean it suits *him*. The words. The music too, but the words most of all.'

Camilla was afraid of what she'd say next, and tried to change the subject, but Prue said, 'I'm going to risk you telling me to mind my own business. And please, never let Jonathan know, he'd never forgive me. I intruded on him, without meaning to, when he was singing his heart out—after you'd given him up. Before that, it was so different. When he came back engaged to you, he couldn't stop talking about you, the way you walked, the way you wore your hair. How your tastes coincided . . . that he'd not thought such a kindred spirit existed. He described a ball you'd gone to at the Trading Post. You'd worn an emerald green dress. I'd never thought my young brother poetic before, but he said your hair was the colour of *manuka* honey, neither brown nor gold. And you wore a scarlet hibiscus in your hair.'

Prue paused, remembering. 'But afterwards . . . he was so silent. Never even touched the piano, and yet as a small boy he used to spend hours playing and singing to himself. One day he didn't know I was at Grandma's, doing some sewing upstairs. I heard him come home, start playing, then sing. I crept downstairs to listen, glad he was singing again. I thought perhaps he was getting over it, until he picked up this song. He sounded so desolate, yet I felt it might get it out of his system. I think he'd come across it, and felt the words matched what had happened to him.

'I'd got right downstairs by then—and wished I hadn't, because I'd never dreamed there could be such heartbreak in a few words strung together. I stopped just short of the doorway. It did something to me, Camilla. His anguish was mine. And I could do nothing about it except steal away upstairs so he'd never know I'd heard and understood. But I dropped the scissors I was carrying. He swung round and said in a terrible voice, "Go away. Just go away." There was nothing I could do except what he'd asked—go. I shouldn't have asked him to sing it—it was stupid, only I thought if you heard it—heard him—it could tell you something. Camilla, it isn't my business,' she finished. 'Have I made you angry? Only I love my brother so and I thought I'd make one bid, at least, for his happiness.'

Camilla stood stock still. 'You haven't made me angry, Prue. In the same circumstances, I'd have done the same for my brother. Only such a lot of water has flowed under the bridge since then. We aren't suited any longer. Perhaps it's just as well Jonathan came back. It's made both of us realise we've grown apart. It's not just me, even if I was the one who broke it off. Jonathan doesn't want marriage with me now. In fact he doesn't even like me any more. He said so, just recently. Doesn't like me at all.'

Prue boggled at her. 'I just don't believe it. You've seemed such good friends these last few days, so marvellous with the children, so united in your care for Hallie, in the business too.'

Camilla made an effort to seem to take it casually. 'That's so, but that's all there is to it. We're civilised folk.' She managed to summon up a smile that, had Prue only known, was nothing less than heroic. 'But I promise you this, Prue, I'll do my very best to marry him off to some nice girl here, preferably with a taste for antiques. Now, come on, love, and don't make me feel too guilty about shattering your romantic notions. You haven't met Greg yet—*my* Greg. He's had a boat out of commission—he runs a small fleet of them—so he's been flat out.'

Prue was the one who changed the subject this time. She chattered of shoes and ships and sealing-wax all the way home, but when they went upstairs she came into Camilla's room and laid a sheet of music on her bed. 'That's it, Camilla. Read it ... I don't want it back. You'll never hear it sung as I heard it, but you won't be able to read that unmoved,' and she went out. She paused at the door, said, 'I would have loved you as a sister-in-law, but if that never comes to be, I'd like you as a friend.'

Camilla smiled mistily. 'You've got my friendship already, Prue.'

Her hands were shaking as she opened the sheet. She read:

'There still are hours of happiness I know,
   When woods and seas and blossoms give delight;
When birdsong lends enchantment to the day,
   And stars add radiance to the moonlit night.

'I take them all and love them all, but still
   I know they lack the matchless ecstasy
That once I knew when you were by my side,
   So dear, so kindred, so much part of me.

'God . . . take my slighted love and hide it deep
   In the unfathomed caverns of Your sea
Where no tides stir . . . so I forget to pray
   That some day, somewhere she'll come back to me.

'I only want to wrest this longing out,
   To stop this ceaseless torment of my soul,
So I may find time heals as others say
   And in the healing find myself made whole.'

Camilla sat at her window a long time, staring with
unseeing eyes at the sea. Oh, how she wished she'd heard
this, read this before she'd spoken those cruel words to
Jonathan. Oh, she knew now she had only deceived herself into crediting him with mercenary motives with
regard to their marriage, to justify her jilting him. She
should have overlooked that lapse of his.

By the time the night of the Ball arrived, the garden at
the back of the Trading Post Hall was transformed into
fairyland with coloured lights. They had them strung
along the jetty and festooned the trees across the water
with them. The men in charge had even made a tall
Norfolk pine into a Christmas tree, saying, 'Well, what
does it matter? It's so near to Christmas. Think how
nice it will be for the tourists who come early.'

Prue was enchanted. 'It seems so unbelievable that
Christmas will be taking place in high summer. I've

always thought of it as snowy trees and Dickens post-cards and roasting chestnuts ... and tingling toes and snuggling down in bed under piles of blankets, and holly and mistletoe and plum pudding. Not warmth like this ... in fact it will be even hotter then, won't it?' She stopped and you could almost see the thoughts chasing over her face. 'Oh, it's just occurred to me. It could have been hot there, couldn't it? In Bethlehem. Yes, I can just imagine the shepherds sitting out in the warm Middle East air, watching that no hunting animals came near their flocks. And enormous Eastern stars, with one brightest of all.'

Camilla said eagerly, 'But some of the traditional English Christmas will be here, Prue. You and Wally must come up here for it. Gran would just love to have little children in the house again on Christmas morning. Yours are young enough to have stockings filled for them. The snow and the frozen ruts in the road will be missing, and people will be water-skiing and windsurfing out on the bays and getting sunburnt ... but it's a tra-dition at Hallows House to have Colonial goose like Joshua and Constancia had at their first Christmas ... leg of lamb boned and stuffed, new peas, new potatoes, waxy and small, and mint sauce ... and always the Christmas pudding, even if it's a scorcher of a day. Our holly doesn't have berries in summer, of course, but the bottlebrush is out, flaming scarlet, and we stick sprigs of that in between the holly leaves and we have our own New Zealand mistletoe out then, only it's not white, it's red, and blooms about then.'

Jonathan looked up from some old brass he was re-storing and said, 'Didn't you know it's a poor season for mistletoe this year? You might have to do without it this Christmas.'

Camilla said, 'I've never known a poor season for mistletoe. There's always plenty of it back in the bush, way in.'

She looked across at him and for once caught his eye.

She shrank from the look in it. It said as plainly as could be, 'Don't hang any mistletoe up, girl. You aren't going to be kissed, even at Christmas-time.'

She said hurriedly to Prue, all unaware, 'I'm so glad your dress is yellow and that our yellow hibiscus is out already. A redhead in a yellow dance dress is just something, and Sylvie says she's going to style your hair so one will tuck in easily and stay put.' Sylvie, Greg's sister, was the hairdresser at Lantana Cove.

Prue said, 'I think it's a charming custom that the girls all wear real flowers in their hair for this ball. You've not told me what colour your're wearing yet, Camilla.'

Old Elinor looked up from her crochet to say, 'She's wearing a new emerald green dress that even I approve of. Some modern dress I can't particularly like, but this is lovely. First time she's had a chance to wear it.'

Camilla said quickly, 'Oh, didn't I tell you, Gran? I've gone off it—I bought it in a mad moment when I was shopping in Whangarei. But I'm wearing my pink, and for a change from hibiscus, Sylvie is making me a sort of bandeau of oleander blooms strung together.'

Elinor looked decidedly put out. 'I think that pink is quite insipid. You're making a mistake. It looks like the icing on the cake.'

Camilla burst out laughing, 'Then I hope Greg or someone will think me good enough to eat! Sylvie assures me the oleander flowerets are almost as non-wilting as the hibiscus.'

Prue wasn't one to beat around the bush, but at least she waited till she had Camilla to herself. 'Camilla, did you change your mind about your emerald green dress after I told you how Jonathan raved about you in the one you wore five years ago?'

Camilla had to drop her eyes to answer, though she kept her colour down. 'Why, no, Prue. It's just that I found out Greg doesn't like emerald green, thinks it's a harsh colour.'

Prue's voice was surprised. 'I think it's a vital colour. But of course, tastes differ.' She left it at that.

The night of the Trading Post Ball was all the organisers could have dreamed of. The Charity it was to benefit was Asian Relief Projects, to dig wells, build bridges, irrigate unproductive land. To New Zealand Asian countries didn't mean the Far East, they meant the Near North. There was hardly a zephyr stirring the surface of the bay waters as the launches began to converge on the Inlet. All the charter companies from Russell, Paihia, Kerikeri and the countless other coves and settlements were bringing their own parties of tourists and residents who didn't own boats of their own.

Twilight fell sooner in Northland, at the top of New Zealand, than in Southland at the foot, where, closer to the great mass of Antarctica, the daylight always lingered. Tonight, it made the scene even more beautiful, as darkness began to fall and the lights of the shipping dotted the immense waters like winking jewels and converged on Reikorangi. Car lights purred through the night from every little side-road, disgorging laughing, eager occupants, young and old.

Elinor looked every inch the grand lady, yet up to the minute too, in a deep blue dress that gave out glints of silver and rose and lilac as she moved. Camilla's heart swelled with pride as she helped her dress. No one had ever had a more beautiful grandmother than this. She told her so, softly.

Elinor turned and caught her girl in her arms; she was still in a cotton housecoat. 'I've been a very lucky woman. Loved and wanted in my old age.' Then she said, 'But I never see you dressed for a dance but I wish with all my heart your father and mother could see you. They had you for so short a time.' Then, with a twinkle in the black eyes, 'Even if you wouldn't wear your emerald dress. Well, no doubt you had your reasons.'

Camilla didn't answer that, but simply said, 'Now off

to the drawing-room, and I won't be long. I want to make quite sure Prue's yellow hibiscus is firmly pinned in her hair.'

Wally was in the master bedroom too. His delight in Prue's appearance thrilled Camilla, yet gave her a lost, lonely feeling too. She fixed the hibiscus, sped along to her own room. Sylvia had given her a superb hair-do. She really was an artist. She had caught the heavy coils of golden-brown hair up high, swathing them round in smooth symmetrical sweeps, securely fastened. A tiny tendril hung down each side of Camilla's ears. She darkened her brows a little, added the merest suggestion of eye-shadow. She needed just a little heavier make-up than usual because of the pale colour of this gown. Her cheeks needed no colour. Just as well Jonathan had never liked her heavily made up. She pulled her thoughts up immediately. What did Jonathan matter tonight? That was over, completely, dead as a doornail. She lifted the bandeau of oleander blooms and pinned it across her head like an Alice-band. How cleverly Sylvie had contrived this—the flat perfect blooms, palest pink shading to deep rose at their hearts stuck on a narrow strip of pale green velvet ribbon with tiny ferns springing from each end. She surveyed her image. Very pretty, beautifully fitting, very ... what was it Gran had said? ... very insipid! She went downstairs and into the drawing-room.

Uncle Edward and family had arrived by then. He was the only one who'd not seen her hair-do. 'That's really beautiful,' he said. He looked at her more closely. 'You look exactly like someone on television. Now who?'

They all looked. Camilla's colour rose a little. Then Uncle Edward said, 'I know ... that Elizabeth in *The Onedin Line*. Remember when that was on? The proud beauty, the imperious one.'

They all laughed, and under cover of that and the ensuing chatter Jonathan said in Camilla's ear, 'How very astute of Uncle Edward. The ambitious career woman, wasn't she?'

Not by one quiver did she betray that she had even heard him. Jonathan said to the company, 'I'm off . . . I'm escorting Edie. Jake simply won't go—thought it was nice for her to be taken, though. And she knows my own partner will be here late. She wasn't arriving in Kerikeri till about a quarter of an hour ago, and she wants to rest before dressing. And I'm to sing fairly early in the evening.'

Nobody asked what partner. They must know who it is, thought Camilla. Who did he know in New Zealand? And where was she coming from? Staying in Kerikeri? Well, perhaps even Jonathan Lemaire hadn't enough cheek to foist any more house-guests on Grandmother. Greg and Sylvie and Sylvie's friend appeared at the open door. Greg made a beeline for Camilla, seized her hands, held her off from him a little and said, 'I won't do all this elegance any harm, will I?' He leaned forward and touched his lips to her cheek, then kissed the other cheek. Very gallantly done.

Reikorangi always made the tourists from other countries feel part and parcel of the scene when they put on a dance, and the Trading Post Ball was the cream of them all. Some of the overseas tourists were positively starry-eyed.

'It's just too fascinating,' said a merry-faced American woman to Camilla. 'This is the way things used to be. I feel I've recaptured my youth. And the way the men— the young men—don't mind dancing with us oldies is just wonderful. Look at that heart-throb there, taking that woman with the beads and bracelets back to her seat. He was dancing with her as if he was really loving it.'

Camilla laughed. 'He ought to be enjoying it. Despite her eccentric way of dressing, she's the best dancer in these parts. He's from London, but living here now.'

'Is he really? What does he find to do comparable

with what he'd be doing in London?'

'Oh, he was in the antique business there and he is here. In fact he's a partner in my grandmother's firm. He's Jonathan Lemaire.'

She'd said it purposely, realising this woman was much travelled and might catch on. She did. 'Lemaire? Lemaire's of London ... why, I bought a fruit basket there two years ago. George the Second it was—beautiful. It had pierced and embossed decorations.'

Camilla nodded. 'I know the type. On scroll feet, probably. Would you like to meet him?'

She felt mischievous. Jonathan would have to ask this woman to dance. Jonathan was charming to her—and sincere with it. His luck was in, she too was a superb dancer. Over Greg's shoulder she saw a group at the door parting to let someone ... something ... in. Greg didn't seem to notice. The twirl of the dance gave her a better view. It was a wheelchair, and in it Morris Glenn. Megan was pushing it, and she had a dance-frock on too, in gold, something that showed up the burnished brown of her hair. Camilla said to Greg, 'Steer me towards the side door, will you ... I want to get out of here for a moment.'

It led down to the trees at the edge of the brook. There was a seat there, vacant, and she dropped on to it. Greg caught her hand. 'It is a bit much for you, isn't it? Having Jonathan here permanently, living in the same house, dancing with him ... oh, it's the devil of a situation. Can——'

She stopped him. 'Not me this time. But I wanted to warn you—Morris and Megan are here. I saw them come in. I thought it might take you off guard.'

'Morris? In his wheelchair?'

'Yes. Brave, isn't it? I think he must have wanted Megan to get a bit of dancing in. Only I thought you ought to have some prior knowledge, not just come face to face suddenly. You'll dance with her, won't you, Greg? Appear to take it quite normally. So many will. They'll realise what Morris wants.'

His hand gripped hers, hard. 'I will. He's a great fellow, isn't he? You knew he won an archery contest lately? His arms are practically as good as ever now. And there's some mobility returning to his lower limbs. Megan has never given up. Without her it would never have happened, I'm sure.'

They came in. Megan was settling Morris in an alcove, and several of his old friends had gathered round. Morris looked up, saw Greg and Camilla and said, 'Camilla, you'll spare Greg to Megan, won't you? Give me a chance of a good yarn to some of the chaps.'

Jonathan answered for her. 'Of course she will. It'll give me a chance of a dance with Camilla.' He grinned. 'Trouble is when you dance with an ex-fiancée, everyone starts to point out and surmise it's on again, so she's been avoiding me like the plague. Come on, wench, let's give them something to talk about,' and he swept her off, to the tune of laughter from the others.

Camilla found herself saying, 'Thanks, Jonathan. That bridged an awkward moment for both Morris and Megan—turned the heat and interest off them and on to us.'

He said to the top of her head, 'You can always analyse my motives, can't you, Camilla? Or think you can.'

That stilled any other light conversation she might have indulged in. Even so, it was sweet to find herself in Jonathan's arms again. Sweet? Well, bitter-sweet. Because it was to be only fleeting. And just a dance, soon over.

She glimpsed Megan and Greg going by. It must have been more than a year since they'd seen each other, but they weren't talking. The expressions on their faces were unreadable. Camilla knew a stab of pity that far superseded her own wretchedness. There weren't any words for what those two must be feeling. Then she saw Megan smile across the room to Morris, saw him smile back as if he was thoroughly delighted to see her dancing and guessed he'd insisted on coming.

For the next half-hour Camilla felt she had no right to think about herself so much. Morris was in high fettle, and she guessed it was because he was so much improved. He was beginning to believe that some day he would be able to walk again. He said to Camilla, 'Oddly enough I'd not have thought of it till someone dropped in and mentioned that Jonathan would be singing a couple of songs. Meg is so passionately fond of singing, and especially men's voices. I remembered him singing *Trees* at that Rotary concert in Russell years ago ... how long ago?'

She said, 'Just over five years ago, Morris.'

'Yes, I suppose it must be. Well, I'd known Meg for a few months then, but hadn't really singled her out from any of the girls in the crowd. But something in the way she listened to the words in the music drew me to her. We've missed out on a good many things, Meg especially, but our love of music we've always been able to share. It was good seeing Jonathan again,' he added, 'brought back a very happy memory. Nice coincidence that he sang that song again tonight. Where's he gone? I want to thank him for it.'

Camilla said lightly, 'Oh, his partner was arriving late at Kerikeri, so he's gone across to pick her up. Nice that she was able to make it at all.'

Nice. That was a word that Jonathan had said some people despised but he liked. The thought of that day rushed back on her, the happiness of it, when for a few magic moments, joy had blotted out older, hurtful things. She had an idea she ought to have compromised, not had such a rigid code concerning that shady deal of so long ago. Then she might never have said that dreadful thing to Jonathan, something that made any chance of the breach being healed, beyond hope. No man would risk marrying a woman who thought he was marrying where money was.

Her grandmother was sitting quite near Morris's chair, and Camilla looked up to see her dark eyes fixed upon her. She hoped no wintry look had passed across her face at her thoughts. She wanted no question from her as to what was the matter.

However, Gran just said drily, 'That pink dress was a good choice, after all, Camilla. The one that's just come in the door would have outshone your own emerald one.'

Camilla looked. Jonathan had just come in with his partner, a tall, dark girl in a dress that must have cost the earth, a glorious green shade with a lurex thread in it that gave off glints of coral. She wore a coral-coloured hibiscus tucked into her hair. Not just a dress run up by the local dressmaker, it was superbly cut. And the girl was Dilys Cranbourne. Camilla's first thought was: 'But when I spoke of her I thought he didn't even like her.' Then she clamped down on all thought about that. What did it matter?

It had been a dramatic entrance because it was between dances. Uncle Edward appeared at Camilla's side. 'It's a waltz,' he announced with great satisfaction, 'and next to your Aunt Rose you're my favourite waltz partner.' The band struck up and he whirled her away. Uncle Edward laughed, 'This is the only ball of the year for me, all old-time dances. Glad they keep at least this one that way.' He looked down on the face of his niece, which had lost a little colour, and said, 'Rose and I were indulging in a spot of reminiscence during one. The Luxembourg Waltz. We never hear it but we remember.'

'Remember what, Uncle Edward? Is it possible I'm about to hear some sentimental anecdote of your past? It might make me believe in things again.' You never had to pretend that all was sweetness and light in your life when you were with Uncle Edward.

He chuckled. 'The lead-up to it was anything but sentimental—the path of true love never runs smoothly, you know. Aunt Rose and I had had a clanging row, and no wonder! At least I knew later it was no wonder.

I had no idea that a very unfortunate remark had been made to Rose. Because of it, when a coincidence occurred later, she added two and two and got about ninety-nine. She accused me of two-timing.'

Camilla was surprised at the indignation that rose in her. 'You, double-dealing? She must have been off her head!'

Uncle Edward chuckled. 'Thanks for that vote of confidence, love. But you see, I wasn't the Uncle Edward you know now, I was just someone who appeared suddenly in her life and with whom she fell in love . . . madly. Hard to believe that now, isn't it?'

Camilla was very decided. 'No, Uncle Edward, it isn't. The only thing hard to credit is that she could ever have thought it. You two have such a good relationship.'

'Now, yes. But for six months in our lives it appeared as if we'd never make it up. I did nothing to help. My pride was humbled. I told myself if the girl I loved didn't trust me, then we had no basis for a lasting relationship. And I was fool enough to think if I'd had the credit for playing fast and loose, then I might as well earn it. I expect it all boiled down to trying to make her jealous.'

He stopped talking because they had come very near Dilys and Jonathan. Expertly he managed to steer her into a more discreet position, continued. 'That nearly goosed things altogether. Rose had just come to the stage of trusting her own instincts about me, had felt it couldn't be true. And here was I, colossal mutt, giving her every reason to believe her doubts were valid after all. Circumstances sometimes conspire to make us give credence to things that our instinct denies, Camilla. If I were you I'd let instinct take over.'

She raised startled eyes to his kindly blue ones. 'Uncle Edward, you're positively clairvoyant! I'd never have suspected it of you.'

The twinkle became more pronounced. 'Oh, there's more to me than being a prosaic old salt,' he vowed.

'Maybe I had a Highland grandmother endowed with the second sight.'

She gave a laugh of pure merriment, the first burst of spontaneous laughter that had escaped her for some time. 'You old fraud! I don't believe you have one ounce of Scots blood in you. Didn't you say once that there was nothing but Shropshire and Devonshire ancestors on both sides, back as far as you could trace?'

'Well,' he countered, 'wasn't Shropshire a great county for witches and warlocks?'

'You absurd darling!' she smiled, and laid her cheek against his in a moment of sheer affection.

She looked up to find Dilys and Jonathan very close again and both pairs of eyes were watching her closely. She was glad. She knew that at that moment she was the picture of a girl quite carefree, enjoying herself.

Uncle Edward led her back to their group, gathered round Morris's wheelchair, and made it easy for her to greet Dilys with just the right degree of seeming pleasure any two old schoolfellows might know at meeting again. Mercifully, Edie wasn't there. Heaven only knew what she might say.

Camilla thought Jonathan might have told her he was bringing Dilys. It would have made it so much easier. She wasn't sure whether to pretend she knew, which would have been natural, or to make some surprise remark. Jonathan solved that for her, said, 'Dilys wanted to spring a surprise on everyone, that's why I kept it quiet.' Camilla managed to say, 'What an absolutely glorious shade of green, Dilys! And the cut turns me equally green with envy.'

Dilys sparkled, as any girl might. 'Yes . . . I had a visit to Paris just before I left. I thought it could be my last chance, so I made the most of it.'

A little wave of dismay washed over Camilla. She'd hoped it might be just a short visit to see her mother and father. 'Have you got the travel itch out of your system, then?'

Dilys laughed, 'I wouldn't say that. It can grow on one, but right now I find New Zealand very attractive.'

Uncle Edward said, 'I shouldn't wonder. Bang in the middle of the New Zealand summer. How are things at the refinery, Dilys? I imagine your dad gets involved in every hitch that occurs?'

Dilys shrugged. 'I've been so long away from it all I've no idea really, though he seems frantically engrossed. No wonder Mother takes as many breaks away as possible, poor darling. I used to wish she'd come over to me for a while. How she would have enjoyed the weekends at the country houses. Nothing quite like a house-party as enjoyed by the English.'

They hadn't noticed Edie had drifted up. 'Like those ones in Hampshire?' she asked, and added, 'I met your mother not so long ago. She was telling me about them. In fact they sounded so glamorous, I'm surprised to see you home.'

Oh dear, Camilla wished Edie wouldn't. That was rubbing it in, surely? But Dilys was a match for Edie. She laughed, 'Oh, those were the least exciting of them all —very formal, too many older people. I managed to wriggle out of them after a while. Some near Oxford suited me better. There was far less tradition with that crowd.'

Edie said vaguely, 'But you fall in with our less ancient traditions here ... like wearing a hibiscus in your hair, for instance. How sweet!'

Dily said with an eloquent look of her green eyes, 'Well, Jonathan had already ordered it for me. I'm staying with the Willises, and Mrs Willis is a romantic and insisted on it, when she spoke to me on the phone.'

Camilla said, 'And it's the exact shade of the glint in your dress. Dilys, we can't promise you anything as glamorous as an English country weekend, but when our guest-room is empty again—we have Jonathan's sister and family staying just now—you'd be very welcome to have a few days with us. We can only promise you bathing and boating, with a few trips to the outlying islands thrown in, perhaps, but it's not too far from Whangarei, and you might like to meet the rest of our schoolfellows again. A dance like this won't give you much time to renew old acquaintance.'

Prue and Wally came across, were introduced. The music struck up again, Greg claimed his partner once more, and Jonathan said, 'Edie has promised me this. It's a slow foxtrot of the Twenties and I've been practising it with her at her place. Everyone's going to envy me, having Edie.' Uncle Edward took Dilys.

Greg said to the top of Camilla's head, 'Well done, lass! But watch out for her. She and Sylvie hated each other at school, and I doubt if she's changed.'

Camilla said very casually, 'Oh, Jonathan knows what she is—he's said so. She came to Lemaire's quite often in London. However, he might like her better in a New Zealand setting.'

Greg snorted. 'Not if he'd known her as long as I have. Even as a youngster she was poisonous. I'm not just biased on my sister's behalf. I remember some really crafty and beastly bits of mischief she contrived later. Odd, isn't it? You wouldn't think, with looks like that, and the money to indulge her tastes, that she'd find it hard to keep a man once she attracted him, but she did. The shoddiness always showed—perhaps it was her jealous nature. She even used to try to break up friendships between two girls. Perhaps we saw more of it. She was a class ahead of you, wasn't she? Well, watch out.'

Camilla said, 'She can't break anything up as far as I'm concerned. It's already broken, Greg.'

They were drifting dreamily in the slow foxtrot. He said, 'It isn't, you know. *You* still care. *He* still cares. I'm sure of that. I don't know what caused the break, but I can't believe it won't come right. Not since I've seen the two of you together again.'

She said chokily, 'I never have to pretend with you, Greg, bless you, and it's such a relief. But if there'd been any chance of a reconciliation coming, I spoiled it all just recently, that night you took me off. Then the next day ... after we came back from our day on the island Jonathan took me to task for what I'd said. He really put me on the carpet, marched me out to the old summerhouse. That alone showed he had no feelings left for me; it used to be a favourite haunt of ours. He was simply furious—and no wonder! We really went for each other and when it was all over I knew that what I'd said to him had no real basis.'

Greg turned her round and said, 'Then in that case you've got to apologise, haven't you, Camilla? You've always been quick to say sorry if you've lost your block. What's wrong with that?'

Her smile was wry. 'Because I've waited just too long, haven't I? I can't do that the very moment Dilys has appeared on the scene. Besides, there was something else. And that *was* true, no mistake about it. He acted very wrongly in that. It was what caused the break.'

Greg looked down on her, frowned. 'Camilla, very few of us go through life without committing some sins. I'm not saying mistakes, that's a feeble sort of word for some of the things we do. I don't think there's anyone who hasn't succumbed to temptation of some sort in a weak moment, or a cowardly one. I bet you have too. Haven't you ever lied in a sticky situation? Or cheated at school? Even if I imagine you've never cheated anyone in a business deal.'

That came very close to the bone. Camilla bit her lip.

Greg said, 'Would you like those things held against you for always? No wonder Jonathan was mad with you if he feels you hold this, whatever it is, against him year after year ... then finish up accusing him of something else. Forgive him and forget it, girl.'

Her eyes shone with sudden tears, and she had to blink rapidly to stop them falling. She bit her lip again to steady it, then said, 'He doesn't even know the reason, the real reason for my lack of trust, for breaking off the engagement. I just told him that absence hadn't made the heart grow fonder, it had simply made me realise it was nothing more than infatuation.'

Greg gave a low whistle. 'Ever thought that wasn't fair to him? After all, justice demands a trial and a chance to defend oneself. Think that over, Camilla. You've been a staunch friend to me. But perhaps the very intensity of your feeling for Jonathan prevented you being just as staunch to him.'

She decided to sit out the next dance, with Morris. What a gallant one this was! He didn't make any of them embarrassed by insisting they leave him, took it all naturally.

This time Camilla and Morris were left quite alone in their alcove. She brought them long cool drinks, a dish of nuts and crisps. 'I wanted this,' said Morris. Camilla was surprised, then she felt a flicker of alarm. She was sure Morris had never suspected. Morris grinned. 'I wanted to ask you something rather personal—something I've wondered about since I heard Jonathan was back and a partner in the business.'

Camilla grinned back. 'Like everyone else you want to know if it's on again? It isn't. That was so much water under the bridge. Only my grandmother and Jonathan's were bosom friends and the two firms are closely related.'

Morris said, 'It wasn't just that, though I suppose it's connected. I really wanted to know if you and Greg are serious? Sounds a cheek, but I really want to know. Camilla, please tell me? Since I've been like this, people are apt to water down opinions to me. Are you?'

She knew instinctively that this was a moment of truth. 'No, Morris. We are really good friends, but we strike no sparks off each other. It's so handy to have a partner.' She managed to laugh. 'Even more handy since Jonathan's come back. It stops people trying to bring about a reconciliation. Tonight I was glad to see Jonathan with Dilys. It takes the heat off him too.'

Morris said slowly, 'So Greg's still heartwhole.'

Camilla achieved a laugh. 'Well, he'd hardly still squire me round if he wasn't.' She dared not ask why this questioning.

She didn't need to. Morris said in a quiet convincing tone, 'In my situation, you can't help looking about when you're in a crowd like this, a circle we used to be part of, and hoping, hoping desperately that in the years to come when Megan will be on her own, someone may be able to make up to her for all she's missed, tending me.'

Camilla couldn't speak for the moment. Morris went on, 'Someone like Greg would be ideal, or perhaps Thurlby Ford. I'd better stop. But Camilla, do me a favour, and don't make a protest when I say this . . . I haven't got a premonition of death approaching, or anything like that, but the doctor knows and I know that in spite of a little mobility coming back to me, my heart isn't really strong. Megan has always shied away from the subject, bless her, but I'd like you to tell her, when I go, that my dearest wish would be that she found someone—like Greg or Thurlby, to give her all that my accident denied her. Especially a family. Would you?'

The sherry-brown eyes met Morris's clear unafraid grey ones in a moment of complete understanding. 'I will,' she promised, and was glad that her voice didn't tremble, or her eyes mist over. 'Morris, thank you for honouring me with that confidence. I won't speak of it to a soul until—until I must, *if* I must. It would be of immense comfort to Megan, I know. And Morris . . . you may have felt Megan missed out on some things, but I know this, she did so gladly, and it hasn't been a one-sided giving, you know. Her life couldn't help but be immeasurably enriched by living with someone like you.' She paused, added, 'Gran has decreed that she and I must go as usual to the eight o'clock service at Saint James' tomorrow morning. She did even before she saw the Vicar and his wife put in an hour at the dance here tonight. During the silent prayer he always has, I'll say a special thank-you for the privilege of having known you. It gives me courage.'

The music stopped, the crowd began to gather in their alcove again. Prue had had a wonderful time. She and Wally danced so perfectly together. She was, Camilla fancied, a little cool towards Dilys. Camilla could imagine why. She would rather have seen her brother and Camilla partner each other. She could well have dispensed with both Greg and Dilys. But apart from that, she'd found it an enchanted evening. No doubt it was good for a married couple to feel completely off the chain and she knew the children were being well cared for by Caroline and Sarah. A fierce envy suddenly attacked Camilla. How truly wonderful to be so settled in life, have a very stable marriage, and most of all to have that sense of utter fulfilment.

At last it was over. The last bitter drop was in Camilla's cup when she heard Jonathan say to her grandmother. 'I'll be very late, Hallie, but I promise I'll creep in like the proverbial mouse. See you in the morning.'

She'd whispered to Greg earlier that she'd like him to take her home before most of the crowd began to leave. Uncle Edward and family would bring her grandmother home. She saw Jonathan's expressive brows twitch together in a frown when she and Greg said their goodnights. Not that she had the faintest idea why. Or cared.

The night had all anyone could wish for in romantic atmosphere, the lighted shipping in the inlet, sounds of music still drifting from the Trading Post Hall, the air balmy and scented with a hundred fragrances, the Norfolk Island pine bearing its garlands of silver deer and rainbow lights, and that glittering star on its very tip, and all the aura of a richly historical place about them. Camilla looked up at the window where the old roadmender's lamp was alight. It was lit by electricity now, and was purely a symbol, a sentimental link with the past. It was an empty symbol for these two who walked up the shell path. They seemed to have no guiding light, no compass. A wave of pity for Greg washed over her. She dared not tell him what Morris had said. The time to reveal it might never come. Yet she longed to be able to let him know.

They paused at the verandah steps, then suddenly Greg turned to her, caught her hands and pressed them. 'I had no idea when I woke this morning what a wonderful day it would be. To think I actually saw Megan, danced with her! I can face a lot of tomorrows after that.'

Camilla stopped pitying him. What was more, she stopped pitying herself. Perhaps, in time to come, she would be given a chance to tell Jonathan she knew perfectly well he'd not considered the material advantages of marrying her, that she had been utterly wrong in that. Even if it meant nothing, emotionally, to him, at least she would have squared her conscience. The other was still something she couldn't understand. It had been sheer dishonesty, smuggling that out, for gain, and *such* gain. But . . . Uncle Edward's words had given her cause to think. Must she always hold it against him?

Greg went down to the jetty area to get his boat ready for taking some of the merrymakers back to Lantana Cove and Camilla let Caroline and Sarah go back home, peeped in on Peregrine and Victoria lying blissfully asleep, turned down Prue and Wally's bed, and her grandmother's, went to her own cool room, its small-paned windows flung wide under the eaves.

She shut her mind to the thought of Jonathan taking the glamorous Dilys back to Paihia, through the orchard-lands, scented with orange blossoms, past the glimmer of the moonlit falls at Karuru and along the enchanting curves and lapping waters at Paihia. She knew the Willises' place . . . it was high on a bush-clad hill, cut deeply into its terrace, and the driveway was arched over by waxen magnolias. Their perfume would be heavy on the air, languorous, seductive. She knew she wouldn't sleep. That every minute would seem an hour to her and that she would lie awake till Jonathan came in. She took a book and began to read.

Old Elinor and Uncle Edward came in, saw her light on, came up. They paused in the doorway. The book had fallen on to her white counterpane. Uncle Edward tiptoed across the room, switched off the light, came back and said to Elinor, '"Sleep that knits up the ravelled sleave of care."'

CHAPTER SEVEN

CAMILLA woke refreshed in body, but heavy-spirited. She slipped downstairs on silent feet, thankful the children weren't stirring and guessing that the girls had allowed them to stay up later than usual so they would do just this. She made her grandmother a cup of tea, cut some wafer-thin bread and butter, and carried it in.

Elinor was lying in bed, watching the early morning sky over the inlet as seen from her window. She looked as fresh as a rose-petal, as if she hadn't been tripping the light fantastic till all hours, as Camilla told her lovingly. She sat up in bed, in a very frivolous nightgown all frills and lace, and said, 'I love dawns and the sunsets more than any other time of the day.' She paused and explained, 'I feel so near David then. Once you've lost the love of your life, the unseen world seems so near. All about you, in the trees and the sea lapping just across the road there, and in the birdsong at night and morning.'

It was out before Camilla could stop it. 'David! So Grandpa *was* just that to you?'

Elinor looked at her granddaughter. 'Just that. Oh, before I fell in love with him, I had a fleeting fancy for someone else—a midsummer idyll. But David was David. Our lives were knit together.'

Camilla said, eyes alight, dispelling the shadows Elinor had marked round her eyes, and giving the lacy shoulders a hug, 'Oh, Gran, you've made my day! There's so much that isn't right in the world, it's wonderful to know of something that was. I loved Grandpa so much, I couldn't bear to think you might ever have married someone else! I still sometimes ache to have him walking beside me, hunting for fossils, or fossicking for shells. He made up so splendidly for the loss of my own father. It can't have been easy for either of you, taking on the full charge of a child of nine. But you never made me feel a nuisance.'

Elinor returned the embrace, telling her, 'We owed you more than you owed us. It kept us from grieving too much, because you can't be sad with a child in the house. I'm glad you still miss him. I read somewhere, long ago, that to linger on in the hearts of those who loved us is not to die. I like to think that you'll pass on to your children, and your children's children, stories about us, just as we passed on to you stories of your own forebears. Now I'd like my tea before it gets cold.'

As they drank, Elinor said, 'David and I made a pact, that whichever one of us was left, that one would feel near the other at dawn and sunset. I don't know which I love the more, but sometimes when the sun sets and stains even the clouds in the east over the Bay I feel that if they just parted a little more I'd be able to step through and see David.'

She finished her tea, put her cup down, said, 'During World War Two, when our hearts were very heavy at times, I read a poem by a Tasmanian woman, that caught my fancy. I don't know if Phyllis Gurney Wright wrote it for her own or for someone else's comforting, but after David died I hunted it up for myself. The last verse went:

'One hour I treasure—pain has all the rest——
You seem to stand at sunset in the west
And gaze across the hills at me and smile.
Then am I brave again a little while,
For then I hear your voice and feel your touch,
As if you told me not to grieve too much——
That you are where those golden acres lie
Behind the sunset gateways in the sky.

'She must have written it forty years or so ago, and still it gives me comfort. Some day I'll drift out there

... on an ebbing tide, Camilla, right through Reikorangi, the Gate of Heaven, and into the sunset. Think of me sometimes at sunset, dear girl. And feel me near. And, Camilla, don't *you* be turned aside by any distractions that disturb your true course. Don't mistake pity for love. Follow your heart. Dear me, listen to me prosing on!' she smiled. 'I'll just wash at the basin there ... no need to disturb the whole household. Hand me my wrap. Nice for just you and me to walk up the hill to church, remembering David.'

Camilla's voice was light. 'Yes, lovely. Jonathan was very sure he'd be up in time, last night. A lot of people are good getters-up the night before, as Edie says. But I guess he was very late last night.'

Her grandmother nodded. 'He was. I heard him and looked at the luminous clock there. It was four o'clock. So we'll move quietly.'

The radiance of the early morning was dimmed a little for Camilla. Four o'clock. It was a half-hour drive to Paihia. It had taken them more than an hour to say goodnight. Oh, Jonathan! As they came out of their gate the bell of St James' church began to ring, silvery cadences falling on this South Sea settlement as sweetly as it had rung in Joshua's village centuries ago. It hadn't always been here. When first the little wooden church had been built, a bell, saved from the wreck of a sailing ship, had called the faithful to worship, but the squire of Joshua Hallow's village in Dorset had had a new bell cast for the local church and sent this out to the young yeoman in whom he'd been interested.

Other gates were opening, people emerging, prayer-books in hands. Some hadn't been at the ball, many had been. The church, gleaming white in fresh paint, in its vertical weatherboarding, so typical of many New Zealand Anglican churches of the early days, had one or two stained-glass windows, but most of them were arched and diamond-paned so that they sparkled in the sun. It sat on the side of the hill, almost dwarfed now by the height of the trees growing about it.

Bright scarlet geraniums and white-starred daisies showed above its white picket fence, and beyond, on the side sloping down to the Inlet, lay the crosses and kerbings that marked the peaceful resting-places of the loved dead, pioneer and Maori alike, right up to the present day.

The Reverend Tom Wakefield, known to all his flock as the Vicar of Wakefield, was standing just within the lych-gate welcoming his people as they came, his surplice blowing whitely in the faint sea-breeze. He greeted them, they passed on up the path, then Camilla caught his voice, 'Oh, good morning, Jonathan. Nice to see you.'

She couldn't help turning, couldn't check the gleam of pleasure that leapt into her sunlit brown eyes, though she subdued it the next moment. 'So you woke,' she said.

He nodded, though his eyes didn't quite meet hers. He said, 'My alarm didn't go off. Good job I shaved before the Ball. I reckon I broke a record for getting dressed. You might have given me a call.'

'I would have done, but Gran told me when we were having our tea that you hadn't got in till four or so. I must have dropped off the moment my head hit the pillow. Gran said she and Uncle Edward found me asleep with my lights on.'

He said lightly, 'Of course Greg had to get people home by launch. Pity for you.'

Camilla agreed just as nonchalantly, but her thoughts were bitter. A week ago Jonathan would have cared about Greg. But since she had accused him of wanting to marry where money was ... or where opportunity was, he had lost all feeling for her, didn't care on whom she might fix her fancy. She'd killed any desire stone dead. And it served her right. Even knowing what she knew he'd done five years ago, and nothing could whitewash *that*, she'd no right to have said what she had. Dilys had turned up at the identical moment to take his mind off it. Even if he'd been rather scathing about her earlier, she was very beautiful, with a sort of audacious charm that could be fascinating to a man. Well, Camilla, you did it and you can't undo it, she thought. Together the three of them went into the church.

As they entered Camilla felt the atmosphere of this consecrated building reach out to receive her, faults and all. She was here to worship, to sing in praise, to listen. Petty thoughts must cease to exist before these associations ... the rough-adzed pews that Maori workmen, learning new skills, had done for the love they had for Joshua Hallows. Some of their own carving, executed with exquisite artistry, adorned the walls, *paua* shell winking back in iridescent colours from the eyes of the figures. There was the stained glass window in memory of Joshua, the one in memory of his wife that said beneath it, 'In loving memory of Constancia Emma Hallows, whose soul was required of her on October 20 1875.'

One of Tom Wakefield's prayers might have been made for her alone. This was the one he said from the aisle, moving among his people, 'Deliver us, O God, from triviality of thought, poverty of desire, waywardness of spirit, and meanness of motive.'

To her horror Camilla felt tears spring to her eyes. She tried to blink them back. She fumbled in her pocket for her handkerchief, but couldn't find it, only her envelope with her collection in it. The prayer ended, the hymn was announced. Her open prayer-book was on her lap, and one shining tear, on the side nearest Jonathan, rolled down her cheek and splashed on to it.

In desperation she faked a sneeze. He had seen the fumble, saw the tear. He fished in his own pocket, produced a folded white handkerchief, handed it to her, saying in a whisper, 'Is it hay-fever? Must be those madonna lilies.'

Thankfully she nodded, used the handkerchief, said,

'May I keep it? I dare not keep sneezing in the sermon.'
He nodded.

The moment passed. She lost herself in the sermon.
Tom preached on grace. He called it the lovely virtue—
the one we so often lack, he said.

Camilla felt every word was meant for her. When the
time came for silent prayer, she asked that when the
opportunity came, she might be given the grace to
apologise convincingly for those words she had spoken
in hurt and anger. *If the right time ever would come.* But
when they came out again into the sunshine she felt
cleansed and healed.

When they came back to Hallows Green Prue and
Wally had breakfast ready for them, and the children
were a little excited about going home. 'But you should
have wakened me up for church,' said Victoria severely.
'I wanted to ask the Vicar of Wakefield sumpin.'

'Like what?' asked her father rashly. 'Maybe I could
tell you, even if I don't wear a collar back to front.'

'Don't you know about that?' asked his daughter
scornfully. 'They're not back to front. They're made that
way.'

'How do you know?' asked Wally.

It was simple. 'He told me—the Vicar, I mean. I asked
him. He was in the Trading Post when I went to get a
lollipop, and he bought me another one, said he liked
children to ask questions.'

'I can only surmise,' said Wally, 'that he hasn't yet
got any children of his own.'

'He has—four. Two of each kind. But they're big.
But I wish I'd thought about the thunder then.'

'What about thunder?'

'How God made it so's you can't see it, only hear it.'

Wally groaned again. 'Why this child doesn't ask
questions I know the answer to, I don't know!'

Victoria spooned some more cornflakes and banana
slices into her mouth and said through it, 'That's why I
wanted to ask the Vicar. I didn't think you'd know.'

Wally hastily changed the subject. They packed up, made sandwiches, filled the flask, put in bottles of pop and apples for the children. The others felt very disconsolate when the car turned the bend and went out of sight.

A tremor of nervousness passed over Camilla. To cover it she said, 'How strange it will be without the children. Children fill the house so well, and this house was used to big families. It feels flat. What are we going to do this afternoon?'

She hoped for some lead as to how Jonathan was feeling. Was he still preserving his anger towards her, under that façade he had to show to other people lest he distress them? Would there be any chance of, say, a walk, where she might find privacy—and the courage— to tell him she didn't know what had made her fling such an accusation at him?

He answered her in a sentence that dispelled all that hope. 'Dilys is coming over. I'm taking her visiting— someone she knew long ago.'

All Camilla's fine resolution faltered. What an anti-climax—to bring oneself to the point of admitting one was in the wrong, then find no opportunity!

Jonathan said, 'I must ring the Casters and tell them. They weren't at the Ball, and Dilys was rather disappointed. Evidently Vonnie Casters and Dilys were great friends at school. You'd remember that, I suppose.'

Camilla shook her head. 'Dilys and Vonnie were a class ahead of me, and you know how it is, a class is a tight-knit affair, stays as a unit even in the playground. But Vonnie I got to know better after I left school. She's gorgeous, one of the most natural girls I know. No humbug.'

'I believe they're out on the Opito Bay Road. Dilys said we could just drop in on them and take a chance they were in, but I'd rather find out if it were convenient. How about you giving them a ring for me, seeing you know Vonnie, and finding out?'

Camilla didn't want to appear ungracious, but said, 'Any reason why you shouldn't do that ringing yourself?'

Her grandmother laughed. 'Camilla, it's a fact of life that men always try to get someone else to do the ringing. You know what your grandpa was like. He never even made a bid to answer the phone at home if I was within cooee. When I objected occasionally he'd say, "Well, Elinor, you have such a nice way with people," the old flatterer. Be gracious, love, and do it for Jonathan. He's never met Vonnie.' Elinor left the room.

Camilla's reluctance was because she was afraid Vonnie would suggest she came too, and she wasn't going to make an unwelcome third. However, that certainly wasn't the case. Vonnie answered the phone. Her voice was warm when she realised who it was, but when Camilla mentioned her reason for ringing, her voice held frank dismay. 'Oh, Camilla, don't let Dilys Cranbourne come here! Not this afternoon above all others. Listen, pet, we weren't telling anyone, but it's so nearly out, it doesn't matter if I tell you—it'll be in tomorrow's papers. I'm getting engaged to Leicester Kane today. Well, we've been engaged nearly a week, but today he's bringing his parents over from Kaikohe and we're having a celebration dinner. I couldn't think of anything more calamitous than having Dilys here. Honestly, she'd take the gilt off anybody's gingerbread! The evening would probably end up by Leicester being engaged to *her*! Well, I know that's ridiculous, but she's a thrower of spanners into works. What in the world possessed her to want to come to see me? I'd have you any time, darling, apart from today, but Dilys, never. I'm afraid you're stuck with her for the afternoon. Thank heaven you rang. Imagine if she'd just dropped in. She wouldn't have faded out gracefully, she's an expert gatecrasher.'

Camilla was acutely aware of Jonathan's proximity to the phone, so she said, 'Thanks for being frank, Vonnie. She did want to do just that, but Jonathan insisted on my ringing you first. No, of course I won't tell her about the celebration. I'll simply say you won't be home. And I'll get Jonathan to take her somewhere different, so she won't catch a glimpse of any cars sitting around the farmhouse. You can see it from the road, can't you?'

Vonnie said 'Oh, bless you, Camilla. What a relief! Look, in a week or two, when the excitement about this has died down, bring Jonathan out here. I'd love that.'

'Oh, thanks very much. Now, I won't keep you. Go and make yourself beautiful for Leicester. My best wishes to you both and all happiness. Bye-bye.'

She swung round, said smoothly, 'Jonathan, I'll have to tell you the real reason, but it's to be kept confidential for another twenty-four hours. Vonnie is having a family engagement dinner tonight. Her fiancé's folk are coming over from Kaikohe, and it's no one but family. I'm sure she'd love to see Dilys another time. Would you——'

Jonathan looked her straight in the eye. 'Oh, don't dissemble with me, my girl. I heard the lot. She seems to look on Dilys as some sort of *femme fatale*.'

Camilla coloured to the roots of her hair. 'Jonathan, I know I fibbed, but believe me, it was only because I didn't want to hurt you, about Dilys. I just felt I couldn't be as frank as Vonnie. She'd have no idea you were within earshot. And she has a carrying voice, I know, though a charming one.'

He said evenly, 'I don't *blame* you for watering it down. I'm only *surprised* that you should feel the need to. After the way you went on the other night, I could have imagined you rarely worried about what you said to people.'

She flinched, but realised that here was a golden opportunity to do what she must do . . . confess she was at fault.

The wretched telephone rang stridently, right beside them. Camilla uttered an annoyed sound, but picked it up and said, 'Camilla Hallows speaking.'

It was Greg. 'I've got to come round to Reikorangi with this boat-load of people, to pick up a party of folk there. At eleven-thirty. We're putting on one of the champagne-and-chicken lunches and doing the round-the-islands trip, home. How about it?' He added meaningly, 'Morris and Meg are coming too. I'm going to lash the wheelchair to the rail. It will do him the world of good.' Camilla realised he needed her to be there.

Relief flowed over her. She'd be away with Greg before Dilys could arrive. She agreed eagerly, eyes sparkling. Before she could hang up, Jonathan grabbed the phone from her, and said, 'Greg ... I was right by the phone and heard that. Any chance you can take another couple of passengers? You can? Oh, splendid. Thanks very much.'

He put the phone down and his eyes danced. 'I didn't tell him who I was bringing. I noticed Sylvie was decidedly frosty to my partner last night. Poor Dilys, perhaps she's more a man's woman than a woman's woman. How amusing! I feel you could truly say of Dilys, why would she want enemies with friends like she has?'

Camilla couldn't help it. 'I don't think any of them pretend to be her friends. Any claims to friendship they leave to Dilys. But I think you'll find I'm not frosty to her. She must feel strange, coming back after some years away. And she's fun when she forgets to be catty.' She hesitated, then added, 'You heard what Vonnie said at the end, about bringing you out to see them. Not to worry. It's terribly hard to stop people coupling us together—they'll realise in time it's purely a business partnership.'

Jonathan said smoothly, 'Oh, don't get het up or embarrassed about it, Camilla. It doesn't worry me one way or the other. After what you said the other night, I've no strong feelings any more. I'll carry on just as long as it suits me. I just don't want any of my family to know what a fiasco the whole thing was. In time they'll accept it for what it is, a matter of shares and profit. I'll live my own personal life on a pleasant level—not a tempestuous one, all emotional ups and downs. After that scene I realised I had had a merciful escape.'

That, of course, stilled any apology she might have made, and though it cut her to the heart she knew she deserved it. The accusation of temperament prevented her from showing any resentment of that. She managed to say, with even a glimmer of humour, 'Fair enough. I know I went right up in the air, but at least it's made you realise this is the way I want it. I think we're civilised enough to live quite amicably in the same house, to achieve a harmonious working association, and in time we'll find all these stupid matchmakers will give up.'

Elinor came in, and from their demeanour even that astute woman didn't suspect anything out of the ordinary. 'How did you get on? Was Vonnie in?'

Jonathan said smoothly, 'She was, but as the butlers of old used to say: "Not at home today." You're as safe as houses, Hallie, with any secret, and anyway, it's only to be kept quiet till tomorrow's paper, but this Vonnie Caster is getting engaged to one Leicester Kane from Kaikohe, and his people are coming over for a family dinner today—very private. We won't tell Dilys. And it so happened Greg rang to say he's calling in for a party for a cruise and wanted Camilla to go, and can take another couple. It's a champagne-and-chicken affair, might make Dilys feel we've moved with the times. After all, she's been a long time in the older part of the world. Hallie, would you like to come or will you have lunch with Rose and family?'

Elinor sighed. 'What's wrong with me having lunch on my own? Cooking it for myself? That's the trouble with getting old, folk don't realise you *like* to be on your own at times. I've never been lonely in my life. Even when David was still alive, I still liked the occasional solitary day. And after gallivanting last night, I'd adore it.'

'I'd better ring Dilys and tell her to get over here pronto,' said Jonathan. Elinor and Camilla walked out of the room together.

Elinor said fondly, 'The dear boy! Did you notice what he said? "Might make Dilys realise *we've* moved with the times too." That means he's now identifying with New Zealand. I'm so glad.'

Camilla ran upstairs, took out her white shorts and suntop suit, and on an impulse shook out the sleek coils of hair arranged so high for the ball, and brushed them till her hair belled around her shoulders, so that it would catch every gleam of the sun out on the sparkling diamond-and-sapphire waters. She made up a little more than usual, using coral lipstick and blusher, pulling a face at her mirrored image as she did so, slipped carved coral and ivory bracelets on one brown wrist, touched some French perfume to her ears and the hollows of her elbows, slipped her feet into the blue and white thonged sandals.

Well, Jonathan had made it clear he wanted no more fireworks ... evidently no emotional apologies either. So be it. If he could be uncaring, so could she. And thank God for Greg as a smoke-screen. That was what he'd used her for once, in a sudden emergency, when he and Meg had so nearly been caught discussing the fact that now she no longer could give Morris up. The words 'broken-off engagement' and 'obligations' had come into it. They hadn't heard the rubber-tyred wheelchair coming. Morris had slid through the curtains, asking, 'What on earth are you two talking about?' Meg, inwardly aghast but outwardly composed, had had a flash of inspiration, said, 'About Camilla, of course. Poor thing, she got pressured into that engagement. Families on both sides feeling how ideal it would be. Hard for a girl of twenty not to feel she had an obligation towards them. She got carried away by the idea of uniting the two families. But once he got away she had second thoughts. That's what I've been telling Greg.'

'Why Greg?' Morris had asked.

Meg had achieved a laugh. 'Oh, just this kink women have for matchmaking. I think he and Camilla would do very well together. But he seems to think she still carries a torch for Jonathan. I ask you . . . is it likely after three years?'

When the ghastly moment was over, Meg and Greg had gone straight across to Reikorangi, taken Camilla out on one of the small launches, where no one could overhear, and entrusted her with their secret. She would never forget the two colourless faces, the quiet resolve of them, as they told her how Meg had been going to break it off with Morris, had felt she must find the courage for it. But two days before she could, the accident had happened which had killed his parents and his only brother, and left him maimed for life.

Meg was going through with the wedding and Greg fully concurred. Camilla would be the only one ever to know. It would help if she allowed Greg to take her out, so Morris couldn't suspect. That was over a year ago. Meg had been even more noble. A month before Jonathan came back to New Zealand, Meg had met Camilla shopping in Whangarei, had taken her off to a tea-rooms, said to her that if she and Greg, after all this time, felt drawn to each other, they were to let no thoughts of the unusual situation that had arisen hold the pair of them back from a happy ending. A quiet happiness emanated from Meg so that Camilla could have done just that, had she had any more than a sisterly affection for Greg, or he for her. But it had never happened.

Suddenly Camilla frowned into the mirror. That was how she had worn her hair five years ago, loose and flowing. Jonathan wasn't going to have any suspicion she was trying to attract him.

She pulled her hair back at the nape of her neck, twisted a rubber band around it, hunted in a drawer, came up with a piece of coral braid and tied it over the band in a bow. Much better.

Dilys arrived promptly, driving her father's Triumph. She was wearing a Hawaiian beach suit in purple and green, with plaited sandals on her feet, and ropes of shell necklaces about her throat. She had swinging hoops of copper at her ears. Everything about her was perfection, a delight to look upon, feature by feature. She was in a good mood, which was something. 'What a perfectly delightful idea, Jonathan. Much better than mine. Visiting is always a bit stuffy, I think. What a blessing I didn't ring Vonnie yesterday, she'd probably have insisted on staying in, and it would've been so ordinary.' She turned to Camilla. 'I expect Greg likes having you along, you're so knowledgeable about the area. It was always a passion with you, wasn't it, pioneer history?'

'Maori history too,' said Camilla quietly. 'But no one needs to assist Greg on it. You couldn't fault his commentary . . . it sounds as fresh every time as if he'd never delivered it before. No wonder his *Sea Pearl* is the most popular of them all.'

Dilys laughed, said, 'Isn't she sweet, Jonathan? So loyal to dear old Greg. Has he never wanted to try his wings elsewhere? Or is the sum of his ambition to be skipper of a boat?'

Camilla was determined not to be ruffled, but said quietly, 'He's the owner of a fleet of cruising boats. A lot of people envy him his way of earning his crust. And he hasn't always stayed home, by the way. He spent a year in the Mediterranean not so long ago, getting ideas. He was in Greece, Malta, Capri.'

'And Sylvie, his sister? Still hairdressing?'

Camilla didn't let one hint of triumph creep into her voice, but said, 'In a way, yes. She'll still be hairdressing after she's married, which will be quite soon. It's a fabulous salon, though, part of a huge hotel complex in Fiji. Christopher York owns it—her fiancé. It's a dream. Sylvie and I had a holiday there last year. That's when it all began.'

She had the satisfaction of seeing green-eyed envy flash for a moment across Dilys's face. She knew a moment of sheer thankfulness that Christopher was far away, though he was the dearest person. Dilys said lightly, 'Fancy him falling for Sylvie! . . . half the wealthiest women in the world must land on his doorstep; it makes you wonder, doesn't it?'

Camilla laughed. 'Makes Christopher wonder too . . . at his good luck in having someone like Sylvie fall for him. He said so to me, he's a very articulate man. Well, I think we'll get down to the jetty. It'll take a bit longer getting Morris's chair on board . . . I suppose they'll hook a ramp-board over the gangplank. I'm so thrilled they're coming. So's Greg.'

Dilys said, but idly, not nastily, 'You know I always thought, years ago, that Greg had a bit of a fancy for Meg. Pity she hadn't felt the same, as it turned out.'

Involuntarily a tremor of fear for Meg and Greg passed over Camilla's face. For Morris too. Dilys was capable of saying anything. She controlled her features almost instantly, but turned to see Jonathan looking at her with a sharpened awareness, a frown between his brows.

She passed him on the stairs a moment later as she ran up to get herself a headscarf. He put out a hand and said, 'Don't let that disturb you, Camilla.'

She blinked. 'Don't let what disturb me?'

His eyes were steady, the first frank look he'd given her since that night in the summerhouse. A kind look. 'What Dilys said about Greg. Don't let any doubts creep in. You seem to fall an easy prey to doubts. I don't believe it. Even if he had looked her way long ago, what would it matter? He's certainly looking your way now. He's a fine fellow.'

She reacted as she ought and said, 'Thanks, Jonathan. That's very decent of you, specially after my outburst the other night.'

But with that gesture of kindness from him she knew that she no longer mattered to him at all. She had ruined whatever chance there had been for a resurgence of that old flame of desire and love.

Certainly it seemed obvious to all on board that Camilla was the captain's girl. She acted as hostess, knew where everything was to be found, and kept coming back to Greg's side. It was good to see Morris enjoying himself so much. It was a dream of a day, his chicken-and-champagne lunch was served on a tray, and Greg had rigged up a little awning to keep the blazing sun off him. Several friends were aboard to chat with him and allow Meg to move about.

She and Camilla found themselves in a private spot at the rail. Meg said, 'Thank you, Camilla. I'll live on this weekend for a long time. So will Morris. It promises him more activity from now on. It's the first time I've been on this huge twin-hulled catamaran. It's the one Greg had built from a Mediterranean design, isn't it? It rides so perfectly.'

Camilla nodded. 'You realise it's called after you, don't you?' Meg looked surprised, and Camilla smiled. 'Isn't your real name Margaret? And doesn't that mean pearl?'

Meg said, 'Thank you, Camilla. That's like having a token of love given one.' She made a small gesture as if her hand closed over a treasure. Camilla wanted to say more, but wisely held her peace.

Dilys blossomed under Jonathan's attentions, and the small lines of habitual discontent disappeared. There could hardly have been a fairer scene, boats tacking to and fro, the multitude of tiny islands with private beaches where children played, and swam, where bronzed youths and bikini-clad girls enjoyed their windsurfing, skimming over the surface of the water on their sailboards, laughing as they misjudged winds and turned turtle.

Hard to believe on such a day as this that there had ever been discord here, and bloodshed, mostly through misunderstandings of culture and custom and the language barrier, but Greg's voice warmed as he spoke through the intercom of the kindness the Reverend Samuel Marsden had shown Ruatara, of Rangihoua, befriending him after shameful treatment by white seamen on long voyages and restoring him to his own island where, on Christmas Day, 1814, Samuel preached his first sermon on New Zealand soil, with Ruatara interpreting.

A fair day, yet after they'd brought their party back to Hallows House for tea and Dilys had departed in her own car while Jonathan went across to their motel with Meg and Morris to help them negotiate the wheelchair up the steps, Camilla was glad the day was over.

CHAPTER EIGHT

EVERY day an increasing number of tourists were coming to wander through the rooms at Hallows House and to shop at the showroom for expensive Christmas presents. Overseas travellers, escaping the Northern Hemisphere winter, came for big game fishing or an idyllic Pacific holiday at, as they said, the uttermost ends of the earth.

The last of the grapefruit, oranges, mandarines and tangelos were piled in gold and orange profusion at all the wayside stalls at orchard gates, selling so cheaply, people from the Far South found it incredible. A few tamarillos still glowed redly in their plastic bags, but the kiwi fruit, green and furry, were long since done. Tomatoes and beans began to overflow the stalls and the shops displayed glamorous beach wear, camping gear, underwater diving equipment, fishing tackle.

Jonathan and Camilla took little time off except for water-skiing from Uncle Edward's boats when they weren't hired, or from Greg's when he was free. Meg and Morris were back in Whangarei, but Dilys and her mother were offered the loan of a house less than a mile from Hallows Green, by friends who didn't want it standing empty when they were overseas. Greg groaned when he heard that. Jonathan didn't comment, merely smiled thoughtfully, and though he didn't neglect his work, he and Dilys were often out in the evenings. If Greg could get round in his boat from Lantana Cove, which was shorter than by road, they made up a foursome, but Camilla refused to do this often.

She said to Jonathan, 'Back me up if I refuse when Gran urges me to go out more. We're so busy all day I feel I must spend the evenings with her. It's not fair on Aunt Rose otherwise. I love my stay-at-home evenings

141

when Greg's out with moonlight cruises. I don't know how long I'll have Gran now.'

He said, 'I can understand that. We feel that about Grandpa and Grandma, though at least they have each other. I would have liked them to come out here for another visit before they're past it, because it is, after all, where Grandma was born. They had thought they might——' He stopped.

She looked at him curiously. 'You mean they were considering another trip? Then what's stopping them? You said when you got that last letter from them that they were both as fit as can be.'

He looked at her across the rosewood table he was polishing and said deliberately, 'Surely you can guess? They planned to come if a reconciliation had come off— for the wedding. I've told them it's no go, so they've no heart for it now.'

She felt herself tighten. 'That's mean! It makes me feel guilty. One doesn't marry to suit other people.'

How calm his voice was, how reasonable. 'Of course not, but you asked. You didn't need to feel guilty. It rests with me as well as with you. I came out here with supreme confidence that I could win you all over again. That was why I took out shares—not expediency in a financial sense, but because that way I could stay and you couldn't bolt as you did once before. But I've no desire for making up now. You killed that desire stone dead. There are enough risks in marriage as it is. I can't think of one much worse than marrying a woman who believed from the start that it was a matter of dollars. I can only think it's all those historical novels you read where heiresses and princesses are married off for their fortunes or their kingdoms.' He actually snorted. 'It's so ridiculous! Lemaires' of London could buy up Hallows Antiques three times over.'

Stung, Camilla replied hotly, 'I daresay they could, but then *we* don't believe in profiteering!'

The next moment she was afraid of his reaction, but

instead he looked at her with cold dislike and said,
'Utter nonsense. I'm not even taking umbrage because
we're known in a much larger world than yours ... all
over Europe and America too, for integrity. I can
recognise your remark for what it is ... you're trying to
justify your childish outburst that night in the summerhouse. Just forget your complexes and weird notions,
Camilla—I'm tired of them. But do treat Greg better
than you treat me. I don't suppose his business really
compares with Hallows—don't ever suggest to *him* that
his courtship of you is to feather his own nest.'

Camilla turned and walked out of the showroom, lest
she be betrayed into revealing her knowledge of that
underhanded deal all those years ago.

That night Greg took her for the River Walk. It was
extremely beautiful, winding over a hayfield first, to the
southern bank, through the close-growing New Zealand
bush that was really forest, with trees making a green
canopy overhead, tree-ferns curving in delicate sym-
metry above their heads too, foxgloves and pennyroyal
and wild daisies scenting the way, and at times leading
high above the river. The air was full of birdsong and
the rustle of wings.

Occasionally side-paths led to lookouts fashioned by
the local council with rough rustic seats set at vantage
points to see miniature rapids or waterfalls. Greg said,
'We won't go as far as the big falls, Camilla, because
there are usually people there. I want to talk to you
about something.'

They found a fallen tree nailed to two stumps, with
another for a back-rest nailed to two more. 'Will this
do? Is it about Meg?'

'In a way. You know Sylvie's getting married soon
... well, of course you do, seeing you're going to be a
bridesmaid. Christopher has been on the phone to me
once or twice lately, from Fiji. He thinks it's a big thing
taking Sylvia over there without a soul of her own near

her. There's a grand opening for someone like me, running a fleet of boats. It's on the very island where his hotel is situated, in fact part of the same complex, though owned separately. The owner is retiring shortly, and I've got an option on it, as from today. I rang Chris from Russell when I was there, it's less public than going through this exchange. I wanted you to be the first to know, as it could affect you a little as we've used each other as smokescreens. Quite frankly, I can't stand being so near Meg any longer and being able to do nothing for her. I had the feeling at the Ball that I could give myself away very easily . . . and to hurt Morris is unthinkable.'

Camilla's eyes misted over. 'Oh, Greg, there are times when I just can't bear it for you or for Meg. But I think this is very wise. I've longed for you to get away, only boats and tourists seem to be your life. This could be ideal . . . at least, I mean as ideal as it can be in the circumstances.'

He said, rather awkwardly, 'The only thing is that it'll make it look as if you've been ditched. It won't hurt your pride, will it?'

For some reason that made her burst out laughing, which reassured him. 'Oh, Greg, it's got its funny side. People will just say: "Serves her right. She jilted Jonathan, now she knows what it's like," and what Edie will say, goodness knows! There's just one thing, Greg, don't let Sylvie ask me over for a holiday or it'll be said I'm chasing you.'

They talked over this aspect of it as they came through the goats' paddock, and into the side-door of the drawing-room, laughing, to find Mrs Cranbourne and Dilys with Jonathan and Elinor, and, almost inevitably, Edie. Camilla had tripped over a loop of clematis on the step and Greg had caught her hand, so they looked the picture of a devoted twosome.

Mrs Cranbourne narrowed her eyes. 'Why, hullo, you two. How well you look, how glowing. What a glorious spot this is. No wonder you want to go roaming in the gloaming.'

For once Camilla felt grateful to a Cranbourne, after what Jonathan had said to her earlier. She dropped her eyes, said, 'Yes, I can understand the tourists envying us. A woman said to us just yesterday, "How truly delightful to have all this to wander in when you step out of your door." She said she came from an industrial centre somewhere.' Then something impelled her to say: 'Yet other places have their own beauty. When Jonathan's grandmother was writing to Gran last April she said that at times she thought spring came just as beautifully to London parks as to Reikorangi.'

She caught a flash of pleasure on Jonathan's face and the small moment lightened her heart out of all proportion. She must remember Jonathan wasn't born here, that London was his home. He'd left all that for what? If she had never known about his perfidy in the matter of the acquisition of the *mere* would she ever have doubted his motives in other things?

Mrs Cranbourne sounded archly indulgent as she said, 'Look at Camilla ... she's gone into a daydream. Perhaps the roaming in the gloaming accounts for that.'

Edie said nothing, which was remarkable, but when Camilla said, 'I must make some coffee, nothing like fresh air for making one hungry,' Edie rose. 'I'll help you, Camilla,' and went out with her.

Edie pushed her jangling bracelets up her arms, removed one floating scarf and said, 'I dislike that woman even more when she's being sweet than when she's being catty. It all boils down to spite, anyway.'

'Why, what was spiteful about that?'

Edie said, 'Oh, come, you aren't stupid. At least you're very stupid about some things, Jonathan for instance, but surely you've got her measure. She wants to underline the friendship you and Greg enjoy, wants to make it romantic. It's wishful thinking on her part. I feel a bit sorry for her. She'd like to see Dilys marry. It happens over and over again—Dilys attracts and then loses out. It's because, fundamentally, she's a poor type, beautiful but selfish to the core, and most men see through her after a while. Often that kind marry some poor besotted fellow and ruin his life, but fortunately Dilys is so transparent she puts them off before they can utter. If you had any sense, my girl, you'd save Jonathan from her clutches.'

Why was it impossible to take offence at Edie? Perhaps because there was an underlying simplicity in her that cut the corners?

Camilla said hopelessly, 'I wish he *would* marry someone, then all my dangerous friends would stop thinking he was my destiny.'

All the bangles slid down Edie's arm again as she banged her fist on the bench. 'You've used the right word, idiot child—*destiny*. Some things are foreordained. And this attachment you have with Greg is about as exciting as blancmange with prunes!'

They looked up to see Elinor in the doorway. She merely said, 'While you were out today I made some almond fingers, the ones with the baked icing. You could put some of those out.' She twinkled and added, 'And do refer to my having made them. That woman has said three times tonight, "Fancy . . . at *your* age." I could strangle her!'

Edie said, 'Leave her to me. I'll fix her.' She didn't need to.

Greg and Jonathan were talking about water-skiing and windsurfing. Greg said, 'Heaven help us if Mother's not taken it up—windsurfing. Just in their own bay so far. They had friends there and while Dad and the husband went after rock-oysters, Mum tried out the youngsters' board. When Dad rounded the point and saw Mum skimming towards him standing on the board, with a taut sail, he nearly had a fit. Now he's narked because he's a duffer at it and she's a natural.' He looked at Elinor. 'How about you trying it, Hallie? I'll take you over one day soon.'

Mrs Cranbourne gasped, 'Oh, you're joking!'

Greg looked puzzled, 'Why should I be? Anyone who still water-skis is capable of windsurfing. The sea's been Hallie's element all her life, like Camilla's is. Let's make it Saturday, Hallie? Like to come along, Mrs Cranbourne, and you, Dilys? You could have a go, too.'

Their refusal was a duet. Saturday wouldn't suit. Camilla wouldn't look at Greg. He was being naughty. He knew very well Gran wouldn't attempt this. He also knew Dilys hated being outshone in anything. She even preferred sunbathing to swimming—so much easier to remain looking decorative. She missed a lot of fun. Camilla began to steer the conversation to other topics, suddenly sorry for Dilys.

Did her unfortunate manner spring from the inner realisation that she antagonised people? Did the fact that she claimed close friendship with so many people mean she'd never had a bosom friend? She asked her about certain shops in London, tourist attractions on the Continent, and Dilys grew quite animated. Camilla almost enjoyed it herself and she thought Jonathan wore an approving expression.

The phone rang and she answered it. 'Oh, Sylvie. Did you want Greg?' Then she said, 'What? As soon as that? Well, yes, Mrs Marsh has started the dresses, as you know, because she's going to be away in January. Oh, how lovely! I don't blame Christopher one bit. Why wait? Greg's looking curious. Just a minute, I'll tell him.'

She turned, eyes sparkling. 'She's had a ring from Fiji. Chris can't wait till March, he wants the wedding in three weeks—said he can't take the thought of Christmas without her and it's their busy season then, so he can't come here. Airini and I are to spur the dressmaker on, and of course, as arranged, you're best man, Greg, but Chris's friend can't make the earlier date, so he'll rely on you to get someone. He says I must have an escort, the second bridesmaid. Will do?'

Greg nodded. 'Tell her it's the best thing I ever heard. No, give me the phone, I'll tell her myself.'

As he took it he said in a low tone, 'I'll tell her the other matter is finalised.' Jonathan was sitting very near. She wished Greg wasn't going to make his future plans so publicly known. It would be better to try to sell his own boats privately first. She needn't have worried, he was very discreet. He just said, 'Sis, this is really sensible. You needn't worry about me. No, I will not get Mum and Dad across to housekeep. I won't be on my own long. Yes, I'm going to do just that. Make you happy? Then it's a good show all round. You'd better get on to the caterers and the Vicar right away. I'll sail over to the island to tell the parents tomorrow. I guess they'll come across to the Cove pronto to set things humming. Goodnight, Sylvie, and in case you're asleep when I come in, God bless.'

Camilla, pursuing her be-nicer-to-Dilys policy, was showing her an early painting of Whangarei in the show-room after the coffee, when Dilys said, 'What's he like, this Christopher? Typical business executive, well fed and sleek? Possibly a lot older than Sylvie? I mean, with a business like that he must have been at it a good many years.'

Camilla suppressed an inward chuckle and said demurely, as one not wanting to disparage, 'Well, let's say he's very mature. And winsome with it.'

'H'm, I thought so. Well, you can't have everything, can you? At least she'll have financial security.'

Dilys and Mrs Cranbourne departed in the car and Jonathan walked Edie home. Gran and Camilla washed the cups. Camilla was just going upstairs when Elinor paused, said, 'By the way, you know those ruby drop-earrings I was leaving to Edie in my will if I predeceased her? I gave them to her tonight. Her heart's in the right place, really, and I might as well have the pleasure of seeing her wear them. She suits any dingly-dangly things.'

Camilla sat down on the stairs and gave way to peals of laughter. Really, Gran and Edie were priceless! Had Gran given Edie the earrings because of what she'd said about Jonathan being Camilla's destiny, or for Edie's threat to fix Mrs Cranbourne for her stress on Gran's age? Greg must have noticed the disparagement . . . with his nonsense about windsurfing. Gran hadn't been on water-skis for more than a decade! Then she thought of the shock Dilys was going to get when she saw Christopher York with his film-star looks, his superb physique and his absolute adoration of Sylvie, to say nothing of the fact that he wasn't a day over thirty. Again delicious laughter swept over her.

Gran was staring, then her face softened. Just as Jonathan came in she said, 'Well, child, it does me good to hear you laugh like that, in the good old way. It's a long time since this house echoed to your old brand of mirth.'

Jonathan stood surveying them. 'And why shouldn't she be happy tonight,' he commented rather than asked, 'with surroundings like this, and the promise of a happy future.'

He went upstairs. Gran waited till she heard him shut his door and said, 'But *he* doesn't feel like laughing.'

Camilla got up, went to her grandmother and kissed her. 'Darling, if I *had* got engaged to Greg, you'd have been the first to know. That isn't what Greg was telling Sylvie. It was something entirely different, but it's confidential as yet, because it's to do with business. He certainly wouldn't want the Cranbournes or Edie spreading it round—it's too soon, that's why he put it as he did.'

'Well, thank you for telling me, but it was obvious what Jonathan thought. Why didn't you say as much to him?'

Camilla looked very like her grandmother as she said, very drily, 'It won't hurt him to think just that.'

Elinor pursed her lips. 'That sounds like pride, and it's a pity. Though come to think of it, why should it? *You* hurt *his* pride when you gave him up. So what's the idea of——'

Better be honest. 'It could be, now, that *my* pride is hurt, Gran. Darling, don't worry about me. Very recently Jonathan told me that any desire he ever had for a reconciliation is all washed up, and he meant it. So accept that, Gran. You're crying for the moon.'

Suddenly Gran chuckled, a wickedly mirthful sound. 'If you can still hurl things like that at each other, I won't give up yet! When you get to over eighty, you can read between the lines of words said in temper.'

Camilla grinned. 'Okay, I ought to know better than to argue with you. But this time you're on the losing side.'

What Camilla said to Greg when she knew he'd asked Jonathan to stand in as groomsman should have blistered his ears, but he did nothing but laugh. 'Look, you work with him, live in the same house, sit in the same church pew, cook his breakfast . . . what's wrong with hanging on his arm while a few photos are being taken?'

She gritted her teeth. 'I do these things because I have to. Because my grandmother pulls the strings that make the puppets dance—at least she does in all things save one, and in that she'll never win. But our associations are purely business. That's our livelihood. I asked Jonathan to get a flat and he refused. I've kept asking him, even told him of an ideal one, but he said Uncle Edward wanted him at Hallows House because it's full of treasures, so it's safer. It would look pretty stupid to occupy two pews under those circumstances, wouldn't it?'

'Granted, but once or twice I've thought he could have gone on a foraging-for-antiques expedition by himself and you've seemed only too keen to accompany him. It's made me wonder.'

'I've my own reasons for that,' said Camilla crossly.

'That's no answer, my girl, and well you know it.'

Camilla had an inspiration. 'Airini is my best friend. I could suggest to her we swap places, then I could take *your* arm.'

'That's just not on. Airini was asked to be chief bridesmaid months ago. After all, she's our cousin . . . and a close one. You know our mother and Aunt Laura were twins. It can't be done.'

'You have all the answers, haven't you? Well, I'll give myself the satisfaction of telling Jonathan I tried to switch.'

But there wasn't any satisfaction in it. Jonathan just said, 'Simmer down. Don't make a thing of it. It doesn't even matter.'

That made her, inwardly, madder than ever. She'd jolly well show them how serene and uncaring she was! She'd go placidly on.

However, she was to find life rarely pursues an even tenor for long. Not all the days were filled with joyous wedding preparations. The phone rang early one morning, as Jonathan was fixing Hallie's tray. Camilla answered. She didn't recognise Meg's voice at first; there was no expression in it. 'Camilla, I've got to tell you in plain words. Morris had his happy release an hour and a half ago. So peacefully. Yes, it was very sudden. I woke and went out to get his early tea. When I came back with it he just said, "I won't be wanting that, Meg. It's come—my time."'

She swallowed, then went on: 'He said that quite clearly, then it was just a whisper. He added, even smiling, "Thank you for it all. Camilla has a message for you—haven't enough breath left to tell you myself. Thanks, love," and he'd gone. A wonderful ending to a wonderful life. Camilla, did you know something that I didn't?'

'Only that he knew his heart was weaker. The other

I'll tell you face to face. It was ... in a very lovely way ... wishing you a happy future, Meg. So typically Morris. Is there anything I can do, dear?'

'Yes, please. Tell Greg for me—soon. But personally, not over the phone. Tell him not to come over till this afternoon. I feel this morning belongs to Morris. I called the doctor at once, of course, but asked him to give me half an hour alone with Morris before he rang even our minister. I wanted to remember his courage and his patience. I'll be all right, Camilla, tell Greg the minister is coming up the path right now. He and Morris were such pals. Be sure to come with Greg, won't you? Goodbye for now.'

Jonathan hadn't moved, and had guessed. 'He's gone?'

She nodded, not trusting her voice. He crossed to her, took her hands, said, 'We all know it's a happy release, but I believe he was such an inspiration to the whole community, he'll be greatly missed.'

She lifted eyes bright with unshed tears. 'I'm going to the Cove to tell Greg. Meg asked me to.'

He was surprised. 'Why not by phone? Oh, sorry— stupid of me. Naturally Greg's the one to comfort you on the loss of so dear a friend.' He paused, said in a tone she couldn't analyse, 'Once that would have been my role. I will forget.'

An awkward pause followed. Then in the light of what had just happened, Camilla felt an urge to be sincere. 'That's not my reason for going, Jonathan. It's because Meg asked me to do just that, and to go on to Whangarei with him this afternoon.'

'Do you want company, or would you rather I held the fort here?'

'I'd rather you held the fort, but thank you. Sylvie will be upset. She thought Morris was so much better she wondered if he and Meg might be able to fly to them in Fiji for a holiday soon.'

Jonathan said, 'Yes, I knew that.'

She was surprised. 'You knew? Did Morris tell you when Greg took us on the catamaran?'

'No, when I went to their motel with them after the Ball.'

'The night of the Ball? Why, I thought you——'

'Didn't you know? Meg told me what steep steps it had. Not like the ramp they have at home. She thought I was odd man out and didn't have a girl to escort home. She hadn't realised I'd asked Dilys. The Willises' next-door neighbours were there and took her home, so on an impulse Meg asked me to stay a while—she thought Morris was over-stimulated and needed to unwind before he'd sleep. I thought Hallie would have told you. I didn't get in till after four.'

Camilla said hurried, 'I was fast asleep when Gran and Uncle Edward got in. And it so happened your sister and her husband had a moonlight dander by the shore.'

'I see. I unwound too. Morris and I found we'd both visited some out-of-the-way spots in Belgium and the Netherlands. He'd travelled extensively before he got engaged.' He smiled. 'I'm glad he told Meg what he did . . . that he'd loved seeing her dancing again. Now, finish your toast,' he ordered. 'I'll pour you some fresh tea. You look as if you need it. Then go.'

Greg was no less than magnificent. His only thought was for Meg. 'I won't see her alone,' he said. 'You must stay with me. It could upset her if I see her alone. She'll know how I feel.'

Sylvie's day was crammed with appointments she couldn't leave to her girls, but she took Camilla aside. 'Would you tell Meg that in a month or two, when she's settled everything, we'd like her to come out to Fiji for an indefinite period? We could find her a job in the complex. She has no idea Greg is buying that launch business—but it would mean she'd be there when he arrives.'

Camilla was startled. 'You knew how they——'

'I knew, but like you I said nothing to anyone. I felt I mustn't talk it over with even you. Now goodbye, pal, and thanks for all you've done for my brother.'

Camilla conveyed the message to Meg, who accepted the offer very naturally. 'But not too soon after they're married. Sylvie has been so sweet. She's never discussed it with me, but kept in touch with me when Greg felt he mustn't come. Mother and Father are arriving from Invercargill tomorrow, and I'll go back with them to sort myself out. If I'm at the wedding people may feel embarrassed at meeting me so soon, and no shadow must fall on Sylvie's joy. As for Morris . . .' she paused, then said softly, 'do you remember that Negro spiritual Edie's husband used to sing? . . . "I'm goin' to walk all over God's Heaven." That's what Morris will be doing . . . I'm sure of that.'

On the way home Camilla said to Greg, 'If I'd been as fine a person as Meg I mightn't have made such a mess of things.'

He patted her hand. 'You were only twenty. But you're mature enough now to straighten it all out. I don't know what it was all about, but it seems to me it couldn't have been big enough to stand between you and Jonathan for ever. Perhaps the wedding weekend . . . the atmosphere of it, will bring that about.' She doubted that.

She was human enough to be glad Dilys wasn't to be a wedding guest, though she was invited to the pre-wedding party the other cruise firms put on for Sylvie and Christopher. Chris's plane had been delayed, the tiny one that came up from Auckland to Waitangi, and so in fairness to their guests, Sylvie wasn't meeting him, but was on the decorated houseboat to receive them and explain the delay.

To Camilla's gratification she was with Dilys when Christopher York first dawned on Dilys's sight. A dance had just ended when he ran lithely up the gangway, impeccable in a tropical suit, ideal for this starry and hot Northland evening.

Dilys clutched Camilla's arm. 'Tell me, who's the dream-dust hero just come aboard? What a heart-throb! Just our luck if he's a passing tourist.'

Camilla laughed back. 'Just our luck that Sylvie saw him first . . . or to be more accurate, that *he* saw *her*! That's the bridegroom!'

It was the wedding of the year in Reikorangi. They called it The Jacaranda Wedding because the trees bordering the path up from the lych-gate of St James' Church were in their full lilac-coloured blossom and Airini and Camilla had mauve silk panniers over their dresses of cream watered silk that were replicas of the bride's dress, that had in turn been patterned on an antique gown in the Hallows showroom. But where Sylvie wore pearls to match the all-cream of hers, they wore amethysts in pendants and earrings, and on the cream satin ribbons that were threaded through the ivory-backed prayerbooks they carried were fastened mauve hibiscus flowers.

Sylvie, as befitting her calling, had surpassed herself with the styling of Airini's shining black tresses and Camilla's honey-gold ones. Airini's fiancé was there, looking very proud of her, and, as Airini remarked, 'Even my grandmother approves of him, praise be, and is taking all the credit for it, because she says if I hadn't gone off to escape her matchmaking, I'd never have met Dennis. Can you beat it?'

But now it was all over. It had been an enchanted day, with the Vicar of Wakefield in splendid form, and the tourists making a large crowd outside the church to see the bridal party emerge.

Edie, as usual, said all the wrong things, like to Jonathan and Camilla, 'Never did I dream you'd be a bridesmaid four times, Camilla. I thought you and Jonathan would have beaten them all,' and to the bridal couple, 'Well, Christopher, just as well you've made sure of her, there are plenty who'd have liked to have been in your shoes today, but at last she's going to settle down. She certainly had plenty to choose from. She's got more discrimination than I'd ha' thought.'

Camilla took her to task for that when the bridal pair had passed on. 'Edie, what in the world did you say that for? Sylvie isn't a bit like that!'

Edie adjusted her bracelets and said, 'All the more reason for saying it. When a man's as handsome as that one, it does him no harm to think his wife was widely sought after. It'll keep him on his toes.'

When she'd gone, Jonathan said, 'If ever anyone knows her onions, it's Edie. But she gets precious little credit for it.'

Camilla choked. 'I could do without some of her remarks.'

Jonathan said mysteriously, 'Some day you'll be glad she has the courage to speak. And don't look at me like that, Camilla, it'll cause talk. You know, someone will say later, "I wonder why the fair bridesmaid was looking daggers at the groomsman?" And someone will reply, "Well, it could be because she got paired off with her ex-fiancé" and even add: "You know, he must have been a bit of a rotter or she'd never have ditched him . . . you never saw anyone as head-over-heels in love as she was, when she was twenty," so do keep smiling.'

Camilla said, looking up at him, 'I'm smiling, see? No one will ever guess I'm saying I could kill you!'

The next moment she was swept with laughter, quite irresistibly. Jonathan patted the hand that lay on his arm and said, 'Much, much better. Now they'll just murmur: "The romantic atmosphere has softened her up." ' Camilla looked up and caught her grandmother's eye. So did Jonathan. Camilla moaned softly, 'That's torn it! Look at the delight on her face!'

'Then let that delight stay, for today at least. I loathe people who spoil other people's wedding days. Someone did their best to spoil Prue's. Didn't succeed. An old girl-friend of Wally's turned up at the church and began making audible asides.'

Camilla was horrified. 'What happened?'

'Someone stopped her.'

'Who?'

He grinned reminiscently, and she caught on. 'It was you, Jonathan. How?'

'Well, first I trod on her foot, hard, then under cover of my apologies, I caught her arm as if I was steadying her, and pinched it cruelly. She must have been bruised. I said, "Another crack like that and I'll toss you over that fence." She thought I meant it and just faded away.'

Their shared laughter eased the tension that had lain between them for weeks. Camilla had a feeling that when the bridal couple had been farewelled and the merry-making ceased, that like Cinderella at midnight, this truce would be over. She had to admit she was enjoying it.

Christopher and Sylvie left in Greg's Toyota for their honeymoon and nobody noticed that Dennis, Airini's fiancé, was sitting at the wheel of Jonathan's Jag, a few hundred yards down the road from Hallows House where Sylvie had changed after the reception at the Trading Post Hall.

Jonathan said quietly to Camilla, Airini, and Greg, 'Now is the hour—come on.'

They slipped out of the back door, across the drying-green, and threaded through the currant bushes of the kitchen garden and through the arch in the thick macro-carpa hedge that sheltered the orchard. From here a woodland path led to where Dennis waited. It wasn't without difficulty because, as Airini said, 'These wide dresses were never meant for bush tracks—these panniers need the width of a motorway, and as for these shoes ... they'll be ruined. Oh, damn, that's black-berry!'

They made it, and when the honeymooners rounded

the corner, sped after them.

'If anyone sees us,' said Greg. 'they'll think we're skunks, trailing them to a secret destination. If only they knew we'd been asked! But it would have been mean to reveal that they have the family island for the weekend—they'd have so-called friends calling in off umpteen launches. They deserve absolute solitude when you think they go back to a full hotel for the rest of the season.'

They came to where in a secluded backwater, a small launch awaited them. Chris, of course, was an expert sailor. The transfer was effected in no time, the last kisses exchanged. Sylvie, clinging to Greg, said, 'I'm so glad you'll have Mum and Dad looking after you. This is your busy season too. But never mind, brother, you won't be on your own for long.'

Greg took his car and headed for home. Jonathan drove his. As they swung from the cove on to the main road, he glanced swiftly into the back mirror and said, when he'd satisfied himself that Airini and Dennis were making the most of the only solitude they'd enjoyed all day, 'Are you going to tell me what that last remark of Sylvie's meant? Be honest with me. If it's a secret as yet I'm safe enough. I wouldn't be likely to want to blazon it abroad.'

Camilla felt her heart quicken. He must have heard her catch her breath, probably took it for indecision. Oh, how she wished they were quite alone. Because he was in a softened mood, and this could be the moment for honesty. He said, 'Don't fob me off.' His hand left the wheel, touched hers momentarily as it lay in her lap among the folds of cream and mauve.

She said in a whisper so low she had to lean close to him, 'I will—but it hasn't been advertised yet, so keep it to yourself. In a few months the man who runs a fleet of boats for the guests at Chris's hotel is retiring and Greg's buying it. Chris feels Sylvie wouldn't feel so cut off then.'

He was silent from sheer astonishment, then said, 'I—

I didn't think you'd leave Reikorangi while your grandmother was still alive. At least, not now. Five years ago
it might have been different. And even then, I was going
to keep you over there for only a very short time.'

She shifted even nearer. She said simply, 'You asked
me to be honest. If Greg and I had been going to marry
each other, Greg would never have left here. I know it's
looked like a promising attachment—it was meant to. I
told you Greg had had a shattering experience once.
This . . . our seeming attachment, was one way of helping him.'

She moistened her lips. She must have the courage to
go on. 'Later, it was very convenient for me.' There,
that was as far as she could go.

Jonathan said, 'I think you mean it stopped all the
talk about us possibly making it up?'

She just couldn't say, 'It stopped me showing I still
cared for you.' There were, after all, limits. And certainly one couldn't with two other people so close. So
she said quickly, 'Yes, that was it. But Jonathan, I
wouldn't have told you even that much about Greg's
affairs if I hadn't known you can keep your own coun-
sel.'

The fact that he was whispering did nothing to lessen
the intensity of his tone. 'You do give me that much
credit, then, even while you imputed other things to
me.'

She flinched, then said on a breath of sound. 'Not
now. That you would marry for money—at least I never
did think that. I was trying to justify my own actions,
trying to make myself believe it.'

This was the closest they'd been, yet it was so dreadful
. . . no privacy, and when they got back those wretched
wedding guests would still be milling round and tomorrow afternoon they were all to go over to Lantana Grove
to view the wedding presents. She was to help Mrs
Peterson serve the refreshments. What an aftermath! She
realised Jonathan hadn't replied.

Then Airini addressed a remark to them. 'Aren't you two being sweet, whispering so as not to disturb us? I suppose you thought that on the drive home, we'll be with the whole darned family, even my grandmother. And she likes Dennis so much she monopolises him. She likes his politics, his attitude to work, his sense of family, says she's even inclined to forgive him for not having a drop of Maori blood in him. She said to him: "You are like my daughter-in-law. Laura is a kindred spirit, even if all *pakeha*." She's always appreciated the fact that Mother knows so much about her ancestors. I hope Dennis knows how lucky he is. I love my grandmother dearly, but she is formidable.'

'Dennis knows,' Dennis said. 'She's by far the most interesting of your family, Airini, not excepting you.' Talk turned on the wedding till they got home, turned up the drive and slid into the second garage.

Dennis and Airini were first out. Camilla waited till Jonathan locked up. He said, pausing only for a moment as footsteps approached, 'That's going to make you look as if you've been jilted when Greg goes away. Have you thought of that?'

'I was so glad for Greg, I didn't. But he did. It made me giggle. He told me the whole thing that night he took me along the River Walk, and I told him people would only say it served me right.' The footsteps, crunching on the shells, sounded nearer. She said softly, 'Privately, I thought it served me right too,' and turned as a laughing group reached them to demand, 'Where have the bridesmaids been?'

At last it was over, every last cup had been washed up, put away. Jonathan kissed Hallie goodnight. 'Not too tired, are you?'

She smiled the smile she seemed to reserve for him alone. 'Only a little. I'm glad I don't feel exhausted. I want to lie awake and remember the happiness of my own wedding-day . . . and night.'

Gran was never stuffy, never prim. She didn't mind

saying that a bit in front of her own grandchild; there was no real generation gap there. She turned back, said, 'I married my true love. I did have a roving fancy for someone else once. But when David came, he was the one and only. Much nicer than nursing the idea of loving and losing all one's life. And old scars have a habit of healing. Goodnight.'

They watched her go with smiling, tender eyes.

Camilla had one foot on the stairs. Was this the moment she could tell Jonathan everything? Or would this new understanding turn to anger? What a pity. The day had been all harmony, even fun.

Jonathan said abruptly, 'Goodnight, Camilla. I'm going to take a turn or two outside. I'm not in the least sleepy.'

Well, there was always tomorrow.

CHAPTER NINE

CAMILLA knew profound relief the next day when they returned from the cove to Hallows House for their tea. No more people to meet. They were too late for Evensong, the worshippers had been in church at least half an hour before they finished their meal. Perhaps now could be the moment of confession.

'How wonderful to be on our own,' said Jonathan. 'I feel as if my smile has been pinned to my face for the last thirty-six hours. No time to even think.' His narrow dark eyes met Camilla's across the table. That look seemed meaningful. Had he not thought anything out when he'd taken that short pacing outside last night? She had watched him through her lacy curtains after she'd put the light out. Up and down the mill-stones he'd gone. She had hoped his thoughts were of her.

She wanted just a little time to think out how she would phrase her opening sentence. Could she say something like: 'Jonathan, five years ago, things were black and white to me. I got myself all upset about you smuggling that *mere* of Mrs Moorie's out, and paying her so little.' Oh, dear ... that sounded horrible. But how, how could you phrase it?

The sultriness of the night didn't help. It would be cooler outside. But not in the summerhouse—oh, no. That first sentence was so important. If only she could get it out without anger breaking out between them.

Jonathan had changed into white shorts, beautifully cut, that showed up his tanned skin magnificently. His silk shirt was paper-thin. Camilla waved her hand like a fan before her face. 'I think I'll get into something cooler.'

162

Jonathan said, 'Hallie and I will wash up while you do.'

Gratefully she slipped upstairs, drew out a pair of green shorts piped with white, and a skimpy halter-top in white and green stripes. She couldn't bear anything else on. She came down and as she passed the side-door the cooler air there smote her brown skin. She called out, 'Jonathan, you'll be with Gran, won't you? I'm just going down to the riverside to cool off.'

She went out of the picket gate, saw families still splashing about in the pools where the river waters met those of the Inlet, but she turned up to the solitude of the River Walk. Coolness enfolded her in the colonnades of the age-old trees. There was the flash of wings, and the whirr of insects and, faintly, the sound of a hymn on the evening air.

Camilla knew where she was going: to her thinking-place. This was where she had come when her mother died. Dad had followed her, shared with her the utter rebellion of her grief and loss. When, such a short time after, Dad had gone too, her grandmother had followed her. But when she had had to decide to give Jonathan up, she had come alone.

It was deep in the woods, not far from the Tiwatawata Falls, and because there were so many rustic seats now, the thinking-place was rarely occupied. It consisted merely of two fallen forest giants, very private because here you could get no glimpse of the Falls, and rather overgrown. She pushed aside a tangle of vines. What bliss to have solitude after the clatter of conversation of the past two days! Here she could marshal her thoughts into order and sort out exactly what she could say to Jonathan. That five years ago it had seemed unsurmountable. She'd heard Joe Moorie had been furious, that he'd talked of prosecution. But the distance involved had quashed that, she supposed. At the time she'd felt the whole future of Hallows House and its fine traditions had been at stake.

Jonathan must realise that it had nearly torn the heart out of her to break it off, but at the time it had seemed to her the only thing to do. She would have suffered even more had he been brought up for smuggling it out of the country. But it was so hard to get it all out in an uninterrupted sentence.

Now, with the time upon her, she knew there was no way of revealing what she knew without bludgeoning his feelings. She uttered a despairing moan.

'What's the matter, Camilla?' asked a well-loved voice behind her, and she stood up, looking extremely young and defenceless in her green shorts and halter top, not at all like the poised career woman of the antique trade.

He came over the logs with one big stride, put out a hand to her because she seemed to sway. She *was* swaying with fear, fear of botching it. And she hadn't found that first sentence yet.

He saw her dismay, took her hands, and suddenly the five years that had elapsed since he'd looked at her like that fled. She bit her lip. 'I came here to think out what I must say to you, Jonathan. I'm scared I might make things worse. Last night, when you were so sweet, I could have done, but you went for a walk as soon as we were alone, and now I needed to be alone too, to think up—to find words that wouldn't hurt you too much. And I haven't yet. And I don't think I ever will find them.'

He was holding himself very erect. Oddly on such a warm night his hands were cold round hers. He said, 'Do they have to be words that hurt? Couldn't you manage just three words? Then the explanations can come after, and they would have lost their impact because you'd said those three words. They would mean everything to me. You know what they are.'

They had, without fully realising it, been hearing something during the last few tense seconds—a crashing, a little distance off, then suddenly it broke into an urgency of shouting. 'Anybody there? Help, oh, help!' It was repeated over and over and it came from the main path.

They turned as one, leapt over the logs, and raced. 'It's a youngster,' Jonathan gasped as they rushed; he lifted his head, shouted, 'We're coming . . . on the side-path . . . hang on!' then to Camilla he said, 'D'you think someone's chasing him?' and lifted up his voice again in reassurance.

They met him at the junction of the paths, a small boy about ten, racing like a demon, eyes staring. Jonathan stopped him headlong. 'What is it?'

Camilla recognised him immediately—Albie Dineen. He gasped out, 'My friend Gary. He's under the waterfall!'

They were horrified. 'In the water? He'll be half way down to the Inlet by now. Come on!'

'No . . . he's on the ledge behind it. He's petrified—can't move an inch. It's all mossy. But it can't sweep him over if he stays there. I told him. Come on!'

Jonathan said, 'We may need help. But I'll get to him first. I'll talk him into staying put. You go for help. The church will be out, so get the Vicar. He's a mountaineer, and if you meet anyone else on the path tell them to come. Go like the wind!' Albie fled.

Jonathan and Camilla ran as they had never run before. They felt as if they were horizontal, their feet hardly touching the track, straining forward in an endeavour to see. Jonathan kept calling out, 'Help's coming, Gary, help's coming. Hang on, boy!'

They reached the clearing where a magnificent view of the wide falls could be had, and stopped aghast. Certainly the terrific width of the river here reduced the volume and there hadn't been rain for a fortnight, but there was a horrible overhang of rock on the lip of the falls, so there was quite a space between the curtain of water and the back of the rock, then a ledge like a path-way jutted out nearer the bottom of the falls. There was an heroic account in the tales handed down from gener-ation to generation, of Maoris escaping from another tribe, when one of them, with incredible daring, had led his friends across that ledge to safety, their enemies never guessing that so hazardous a traverse could be made.

Here was Gary Soames, a full third of the way across, above the deepest, most treacherous pool of all, truly petrified, as his friend had said. He was crouched back against the wet face of the rock, a hand on either side, looking through the curtain of water at them.

Camilla felt sick and supposed Jonathan did too, but they mustn't let Gary see how appalled they were. She said, through teeth that seemed to chatter through fear, 'Can they . . . will they get him with ropes?'

His voice was level, low. 'They couldn't, from there. He couldn't reach out through the water—his arms are too short. There's only one way. He'll have to come back the way he got in. But he can't do it alone, he needs company. I'm going across after him.'

Only the tiniest protesting gasp escaped her. They dared not let Gary even sense their own terror. They'd already called out reassurances, shouting above the noise of the cascade. They began again, then ceased, turned to each other. Jonathan said, 'I *must*.'

Her look was piteous, but she wasn't old Joshua's descendant for nothing. 'I know,' she said. 'Oh, Jonathan!'

He said quickly, 'But there—just now—you were going to say . . .?'

Her eyes met his frankly. 'I was going to say I love you, I love you. I always have. Come back to me, Jonathan.'

'That'll bring me back,' he promised her.

He had his sandals off in an instant, his shirt. 'Stay there and keep talking to him.'

'No. I'm going down the path to the wider part below the pool, then if he slips off I should be able to rescue him. It stops seething as it widens out. You know I'm trained in life-saving.'

His eyes raked the area. 'You're right. But, girl, take no unnecessary risks. Till later, love.'

'Till later,' she said as she turned and sped quickly down the path to where, not very far away, the river, though deep, became a millpond compared to that other churning cauldron in the basin below the falls. She waded into the water, tensed to any eventuality.

She had a terrifying view of the ledge from down here, and the blurring curtain of water and the man edging along inch by inch, continuously talking to the small boy flattened against the slimy walls. Her eyes strained to note every detail, yet her ears were concentrated to listen for sounds of help coming.

He was getting there, he was getting there, 'Oh, dear God, keep his feet from slipping. He's almost there ... don't let that boy rush him. Oh, God—God?'

The boy certainly didn't rush him. He crumpled as Jonathan got to him. Fortunately he managed to get a good hold of the boy, wet and slithery though he was, got him into a sitting position, then forced his head between his knees.

The ledge was so narrow, so mossy, so veined with cracks. Camilla's heart was in her mouth and she wondered how Jonathan would pass him to the rescuers when they came. The boy revived, she could hear Jonathan talking to him but not what was being said; then he called to her, 'I'm going to get him out of here now. We'll manage fine. Do your watching, will you?'

That gave nothing away to Gary of what she would be watching for. She dared not protest, scream to him to wait, because it might unnerve the lad. Jonathan would have his reasons. The boy must be all in, couldn't wait for help.

She cupped her hands and yelled, 'I'm standing by. Good show. He'll soon be on dry land.'

It seemed an eternity. If life is measured in heartbeats, not minutes, this took years. Jonathan stepped over the boy to his far side, got him to his feet, put a hand each side of the boy's waist, shuffled him along from the back, and Camilla guessed their toes were digging into any crevice they could find. She thought Jonathan would be uttering words of encouragement as they went.

How she longed to be up there, to reach out across that last foot or two of peril to swing the boy to safety, then reach out a steadying hand to Jonathan, but she dared not move from here. She was the last line of defence if the boy slipped. If only the lad didn't pass out again, slither through Jonathan's wet fingers.

She held her breath, as, miraculously, he swung the boy to the gravelly edge, and safety. Then it happened. The extra weight with the swing forward loosened some rotten rock under Jonathan's left foot. He made a desperate attempt to regain his balance, then, realising it was no good, an equally desperate try to leap to the edge, didn't make it, and disappeared with the fall of the water into the gurgling horrible pool below.

Camilla yelled with all her might, 'Stay where you are, Gary, I'll get him!' and dived from where she stood into the deeper water beyond. He'd be churned round and swirled about, but he was a strong swimmer and would come up, and the force of the water would bring him over here and she'd assist him to the shallows.

She came strongly to the middle, and knew her worst moment when she couldn't see him at all ... then she had a glimpse of the wet white shorts, and his body tumbling over the lip of the pool towards her ... he must be letting it do that to him, not wasting his energy, till he got into the wider reach and could strike out.

Then, with fear, she realised he was being borne along and wasn't going to strike out ... either his lungs were saturated or he'd knocked his head against the rocks. His head came up, and she saw a gleam of red.

She went through the water like an arrow, there was no distance to it, reached him, turned him over, then kicked backwards, out of the main current. But it bore her farther down than she'd hoped ... she knew it was deeper downstream where the river narrowed again, but she made a superhuman effort, felt an agonising pain in her shoulder, but that meant a rock, and a rock meant something to cling to and spelled hope ... she tried to turn with him ... and then, blessedly, muscular arms reached her from the higher side, pinned her against the rock, and began dragging them both to safety. Her nails were biting into Jonathan's flesh, she knew. They mustn't, mustn't let go. She felt a heave, then was flung on to the rocks that jutted out from the bank, and hands were prising hers from Jonathan's flesh. She let him go into the haven of other, stronger arms.

Despite the shingle that scored deeply into her legs, she turned on her front and the Vicar's voice said, 'We'll get him round. We know what to do as well as you. Just lie still.'

But she couldn't. She crouched, watching their every movement. It seemed to her half the congregation was here. They worked expertly. The Vicar said, 'Very little water in him. He must have bashed his head as he was whirled out of the pool, I'd say; if he'd copped it first, he'd be much worse. And you got him the next minute and had his head out of the water. We actually saw it all as we ran round the path. The doctor will be here in a jiffy—someone went for him. Ah, he's coming round.'

Jonathan opened his eyes, stared at them uncomprehendingly, then raised his head, saw Camilla, looked his relief and said weakly, 'Gary?'

The Vicar said, 'He's all right, Jonathan, and getting lots of attention.' Jonathan lay back, closed his eyes.

Camilla, kneeling beside him now, said, 'Jonathan, how bad is your head?'

He opened his eyes and as if he had no idea anyone else was around, as if his poorly-focusing eyes saw only her and the sky above her, and said quite distinctly, 'I said it would bring me back, sweetheart, and it did.

Head's tougher than you think,' and he closed his eyes again.

The Vicar looked sharply at Camilla and smiled slightly, then realised Jonathan was trying to say something and bent his head to catch it. 'Don't let Gary's mother be cross with him. He was so game. When I was getting him along the ledge he said, "Tell Mum I'm sorry . . . if I don't make it." You could forgive a kid a lot for that.'

'You could indeed,' said the Vicar firmly. 'Ah, here's Dr George.'

It was a good job nothing surprised that stolid man, solid as Gibraltar. He saw a shivering small boy, wrapped in someone's cardigan, his Vicar clad in shirt and trousers, dripping wet, a few other people equally wet, Jonathan Lemaire with bloodied head and feet, and Camilla Hallows whom he'd brought into the world, in a soaked halter-top and shorts, with blood pouring from a shoulder, and a great crowd of people in their Sunday best.

He made his examination, bound the two of them up, gave Jonathan some sort of restorative and said, 'I'd rather not wait for a stretcher . . . you men can take it in turns to chair him.'

Jonathan protested that he could go under his own steam, but the protests were feeble. Progress was slow, because the track was so narrow and they met other people coming, as the news had spread round. Among them Camilla was thankful to see Uncle Edward and Aunt Rose. She asked them to go ahead and prepare Gran, assuring them they were none the worse. Not really.

It would take more than that to rattle Gran. Finally, only the Vicar, the doctor, and Edward and Rose stayed. The boys were taken home, and the two injured were dumped on the spare-room beds downstairs. Dr George said something to Rose and she held a pad firmly on Camilla's shoulder. He made a more detailed examination of Jonathan, pronounced himself fairly satisfied though he'd want X-rays, then said, 'And now I'll stitch that shoulder.'

Jonathan sat bolt upright at that and went to swing his legs over the side of the bed, but the doctor restrained him. 'No, you don't! I've stitched her up twice before. She can take it—never saw such a tomboy! But first I must look at her ribs.' He turned her on her side, undid the halter, prodded her and said, 'No harm done. Your shoulder took the brunt. But you'll have a hefty bruise there tomorrow. No one must hug you in their exuberance of relief.'

Camilla's eyes met Jonathan's as she turned back and she looked away hastily. The doctor said, 'Now, I'll get this local in.' He glared at Jonathan. 'Stop wincing! I'm not doing it to you.'

When it was neatly done and covered up, Aunt Rose took Camilla off to change, though the light fabric had almost dried on her in the warm air. Uncle Edward brought some things down for Jonathan, and a pair of his trousers and a shirt for the Vicar too.

The Vicar said, laughing. 'I'd just got myself out of my robes and into a jacket when young Albie arrived. Pauline had gone on ahead with a crowd for supper. The congregation had dispersed but weren't any farther than the Trading Post. I took off without waiting to divest myself of anything, but I discarded them as I went. I can only hope someone retrieved them. Certainly nobody would pinch a dog-collar and stock!' Then, just as Camilla and Rose and Hallie returned, his smile faded. 'I've just remembered I must be responsible for this mad caper of Gary's. I told the children in church that story a month ago.'

Hallie said, 'All the children here grow up knowing that story, Tom. Gary probably heard it first at his mother's knee. Don't whip yourself, Vicar.'

He gave a more cheerful grin, then looked incredibly sly. 'But good cometh out of evil, my friends . . . from what Jonathan said to Camilla when he regained consciousness, I think we've just ended a long-time mis-understanding!' and he beamed.

They all stared at the couple in question, then Uncle Edward chuckled as wickedly as the Vicar, 'Well, I'm blessed! Look at that . . . *both* blushing!'

Camilla wondered wildly what to do. The Vicar had beaten the gun. Nothing had been explained, nothing had been sorted out. Oh, Jonathan, what have I done to you now?

Jonathan took it very calmly. 'Yes, Vicar, it's all on again. Though I shall never forgive Gary Soames for spoiling my happiest moment in five years.'

Camilla looked up and saw the slow tears slipping down her grandmother's lined cheeks. She smiled mistily at her, then said, 'Don't broadcast it yet, please. We—we have some ratifying to do. Just keep it to this small circle here till we do.'

The Vicar was enjoying himself. 'Can't be done, dear girl. Don't you realise half my congregation heard what Jonathan said? Even if our chief broadcaster of such items was missing. Edie went to the Presbyterian service tonight with the friend she had staying with her for the wedding.'

Jonathan said in a firm tone, 'Poor Edie! But I'll ring her myself tomorrow and tell her. She deserves that.' He saw the look on Camilla's face and added, 'I'll tell *you* tomorrow too, my love, why she deserves it.'

Aunt Rose said, 'Now, we'll all have coffee. Doctor, you'll stay, won't you?'

'Too right. I wouldn't miss a word. Most interesting accident I've attended for ages. Further revelations may come. I like my coffee with one spoon of sugar and these two will have some in theirs whether they like it that way or not,' he added. 'Rose, you'd better stay here tonight in case either of them want any attention.'

When they realised Jonathan and Camilla weren't going to be drawn out any further, they made it short, mercifully, and Aunt Rose soon shepherded them off to bed. But before she finished fussing she told them she'd be very happy to hear more details in the morning.

She looked out of Camilla's window. 'I might have known it! Mother is leaning over the gate with the Vicar, finding out, I've no doubt, exactly what Jonathan said to you in public. She won't be in for ages, if I know her. She'll have the whole wedding arranged by the time she leaves him.'

Camilla closed her weary lids and feigned sleep.

CHAPTER TEN

NATURALLY the next day was hectic. Aunt Rose answered the phone practically non-stop, tourists flocked to the showroom, eager to hear more details, but stopping to purchase what ever took their fancy, so Wilma had to call in her daughter to help.

Jonathan rose up from what they called his sick-bed, to phone Edie, but as he did it at the dining-room extension and turned the key for privacy, blatantly admitting the fact, Camilla could do no more than make a small bleat of protest.

When he came out she said, 'Jonathan, I said I'd gone there last night to think things out, for the explanations I must make. But Fate didn't give us a chance. And who knows how you'll feel when I tell you what I heard all those years ago.'

His grin was uncaring. 'Makes no difference to the outcome, dear girl. This time we add one and one and make it two. No wrong answers. It's so simple. You love me. I love you. We can all make blunders. They needn't affect our whole lives. But with the doctor's visit hanging over my head and an X-ray appointment goodness knows when, we'll have no chance for serious discussion. And listen, idiot, you said last night you were scared. That's absurd. I'll take whatever you thought about me, as long as in the end we get each other.'

He looked struck by something. 'You said what you'd *heard.* I'll just ask you one thing before Dr George gets here. Was it anything to do with Dilys? Because if so you can forget the lot—I mean, if she hinted at anything between her and me. The only reason I've taken her out since she came home was because I wondered if I had any chance of making you jealous.' Then he answered his own question. 'But it couldn't have been Dilys because she didn't turn up at Lemaire's till after you broke it off,' he looked up. 'Oh, for Pete's sake, Camilla, here are Mr and Mrs Soames! How do we handle gratitude? How embarrassing!'

As they went to meet them Camilla reflected it hadn't been mischief-making on Dilys's part. The only way in which she was involved was that she'd casually sent on that clipping about the sale of the *mere*. It was still a hurdle to be taken. Despite all Jonathan's confidence it was quite evident he thought it was some gossipy rumour he could dispel. But it wasn't. Old Mrs Moorie had been so definite. There was the fact of the sale, in black and white. Camilla had been glad the Moories lived a distance off, she hadn't wanted to go near them in case it brought Jonathan into prominence for shady dealing and illegal smuggling. The familiar wave of unease shivered over her.

She pulled herself together. It was something she had to forgive, then forget. In that ghastly moment last night when those churning waters had tossed Jonathan at her, possibly lifeless, none of this had mattered. He was alive, and they were going to marry.

Mrs Soames said: 'We weren't allowed to come to you last night. We didn't know a thing about it till they brought Gary in. Words are so inadequate. He could have been washed off that ledge and they might never have found him. It was an ebb tide.'

Mr Soames said: 'We haven't needed to point out that being too adventurous can lead you into trouble and involve others too. Gary's told us that when he saw you smash up against that rock and go under, he knew exactly what he'd done. He never dreamed Camilla could save you.' He turned to Camilla. 'And how you did it, I'll never know.'

She grinned. They mustn't overdo this in front of Gary. Except that it might make him less venturesome. 'You see, I was already watching for something like this, though I didn't dream it would be Jonathan. I was there in case Gary slipped. It was sheer bad luck that that piece of rock at the edge was rotten. Gary had been so game, so obedient.'

Soames nodded. 'Bits of that ledge have been falling off for years, due to the constant action of the water. Not for nothing are they called the Tiwatawata Falls.' He said to Jonathan particularly, seeing he wasn't a New Zealander, 'That name means the Palisade Falls; the whole formation is like the palisades of the fortified *pas*. There used to be quite an edge of them sticking up like a fence. Even in my day they've almost crumbled away entirely. I've said to Gary that those long-ago warriors had at least that protection.'

Gary's lips compressed themselves. 'But *they* did it in the dark, Dad, and they were frightened the others would hear them.' They liked him for giving credit for that, and also that he wasn't swaggering at all, didn't see himself as a hero.

Jonathan said, 'Desperation lent them courage, Gary. But you weren't lacking in it either. You obeyed me in everything. Now, how about going out to Mrs Gidding, she's in the kitchen making coffee, and tell her you'd like to have some Coke? You might say I'd like ginger gems with mine.'

When they heard him talking to Rose, Jonathan said, 'You can be proud of your boy, the way he controlled his panic and gritted his teeth. He must have known my grip of him was anything but secure. It was no more than gave him moral support. And he was icy cold— that was why I dared not wait for help. Plus the fact I'd realised the rock was rotten most of the way and that a rescue party might put too much weight on it. If he'd panicked and refused to move we'd both have been over. Now, if he gets the okay from the doctor, I think he should be allowed back to school. He needs normality.'

They nodded. Soames said to Camilla, 'We've known you since you were a spunky little girl; we'll now always remember that but for you Gary would have had to go through life knowing he'd cost a man in the prime of his, his existence.'

It was a relief to see the doctor coming. He was rubbing his hands together. 'Good time to arrive—I see more coffee's coming up. How are you all? Had a look at Gary in the kitchen, and he's fine. After the TV team's been and gone, he can go back to school. Oh, there you are, Gary. With a bit of luck you'll see yourself on the screen tonight—tomorrow night if they're pushed for time. But don't let it make you cocky. It doesn't pay.'

Gary gulped. 'No, sir.'

Jonathan and Camilla were looking horrified. The doctor laughed at them. 'Met the team in the village, and they asked the way. Someone in the crowd last night phoned them in Auckland. Hope you feel up to being first class news.'

'We don't. The sooner this dies down the better, Doc,' said Jonathan. 'We've got things to attend to.'

'I'll guarantee you have.' The doctor was grinning. He picked up Camilla's left hand, shook his head. 'What a slowcoach! I was sure she'd be wearing a ring this morning. After all, there's a whole showcase of rings in the antique shop. What's holding you up?'

Jonathan grinned back. 'All I need is about half an hour to ourselves to put it on. Show-room rings nothing! I brought the original ring with me when I came out.'

Camilla turned scarlet. Mrs Soames said delightedly, 'Then it's true what some of them told me last night!' She looked saucily at Jonathan. 'What you said when you came round.'

'It's true,' he admitted. 'I don't mind who knows it round here, but if any of you let out what I said, to the newsmen, I'll fly to the South Pole with her. I have my limits.'

Camilla closed her eyes. If only those terrible explanations weren't ahead of her, how heavenly this would be. The doctor shepherded the Soameses out, told them to come back in a moment for their coffee. 'I told that TV crowd to see the Vicar first. I thought he and Pauline could give them morning tea—said I had to make sure you were okay for interviews first.'

He was pleased with them. 'But I've made arrangements for the X-ray. I know it's a distance, but it's got to be done. I'll have Camilla's shoulder taken too. I don't think she's chipped the bone, but I must be sure. You can't drive, either of you. Get Edward to take you.'

So they wouldn't even be alone in the car! Camilla said, 'I suppose you'll have to rush on now, on your rounds?'

He chuckled. 'I've an easy round today. You're just afraid I'll drop bricks. But you couldn't get me away with a bulldozer. Can't let the Vicar get all the limelight. The bounder beat me at chess last week. Here he is now, heaven help me. They've dragged him along too.'

The next three-quarters of an hour seemed endless to Camilla. Jonathan surpassed even the doctor's and the Vicar's romantic ideas. The men scribbled madly, 'Jonathan Lemaire, a partner in the firm of Hallows Antiques, formerly of Lemaire's of London, and his partner, Camilla Hallows.' He was interrupted by Jonathan. 'My partner *and* fiancée,' he said.

'Nice touch,' approved the reporter. 'The public will love it.'

Jonathan encountered a glare from Camilla and went wicked. 'In fact,' he said, 'we'd been engaged only two seconds when we heard all the commotion Albie Dineen was making calling for aid.'

'Peace of the proposal scene shattered by screams for help from Gary's friend. Say, we ought to have him here too. Would someone ring the school and ask him to sprint along? He seems to have been in good training.'

Camilla gave up. She might as well save her breath. Wasn't it usually the women who were supposed to be romantic? This time it was the male element intent on spilling the beans. The Vicar drew the contrast between the scene at Saturday's wedding, with Camilla in a period costume of cream and lilac, and a sodden figure in halter top and shorts the next evening, getting her new fiancé to the bank.

Through it all Grandmother sat, exquisite, un-ruffled, smiling at the inner knowledge that what she had schemed for, and even engineered, had come to pass.

They were spared one thing. Edie had had to take her friend to the airfield at Waitangi, and arrived five minutes after the television crew had left. Had she been here Camilla knew nothing would have stopped her tell-ing them that this was really the resumption of an en-gagement broken five years ago. One had to be thankful for small mercies.

Jonathan went straight to her, took her hands, kissed her on both cheeks and said, 'I haven't told Camilla about that yet. There just hasn't been time. But when I do she'll thank you too.'

They had a quick lunch, then departed with Uncle Edward for the distant hospital. He put them in the back of the Jaguar, confessed he was glad to get the chance of driving it, said, 'I'll use the mirror on the right wing, not the centre one for rear vision. Take full advantage of that, you two. Sorry I'm not conveniently deaf, but I'll switch the radio on, that'll give you some privacy.'

Darling Uncle Edward! But it was still no place for what she had to reveal. Anyway, after a crack such as Jonathan had had, it wasn't fair to inflict such a trau-matic experience upon him, because he was going to feel very guilty. She must remember to tell him she was sure that nowadays he wouldn't do such a thing.

She turned to look at him and said, 'I can only think you might not have been with me today.' She shuddered. Jonathan caught her close, forgetting her stitched shoulder, and his mouth came down on hers in the remembered bliss of other days. He left his arms about her but lifted his head, smiled down on her. 'This is as it ought to be—you and me in a world of our own. Bother the X-rays, bother the fuss and commotion! Don't be scared about anything, love. Oh, look, we're passing the Treaty House.' They were going via Waitangi and Paihia.

'Camilla, do you remember that afternoon we spent in the Treaty House long ago and we were enchanted with that letter that the Lieutenant-Governor of the time wrote his wife when he was recovering from a premature stroke in her absence? I think it was early April, in 1840 just after the Treaty was signed. Forget his name, though. Can you remember the exact wording? I called in to see it recently, trying to recapture the spirit of that day and telling myself it just had to be that some day we'd mend our differences.'

'I know it off by heart,' she told him, 'because we've got it on some souvenir cards. I remember that day. We'd been reading just that week some book that put the former generations as harsh and dictatorial, especially husbands. And here was William Hobson writing: "Dear Liz, I look for you with all anxiety, every hour tells me how dear you are to me." '

Jonathan nodded. 'I'm glad you remembered it. We swore that if a man of his generation could be so articulate, we too would always find words to tell each other how much we loved. So,' he flicked her cheek with one finger caressingly, 'you needn't be afraid. I won't be angry.'

The sherry-brown eyes darkened. 'That won't be possible. It will make you feel humiliated and you won't understand, quite, why it meant so much to me, because unlike me, you didn't grow up among Maoris and so can't begin to imagine what a betrayal it seemed to me. Oh, Jonathan, I'll have to stop,' she sighed. 'Uncle Edward is too near despite that radio and it's just to be between you and me.'

'Right. Not long to go now. Am I hurting your shoulder?'

'A little. Slip your hand down under my arm—ah, that's better. In fact, heavenly.' The look they exchanged was a promise of things to come. 'Jonathan, what made you change towards me the day of the wedding? I thought that night I fired those ridiculous accusations at you I'd destroyed every feeling you ever had for me.'

His clasp tightened. 'Some things are indestructible. And we belong.'

'But what did change you? Not just the romantic atmosphere, I'm sure.'

He said simply, 'Edie did. She called me over one night, said she had something for me and gave me this.' He drew a piece of paper out of his pocket, but held it out of her reach. 'It was like being handed all heaven on a platter. Nothing that had happened between us, nothing you'd said to me that awful night mattered any longer. I knew you'd always written a little bit of poetry. This wouldn't have meant a thing had you written it *before* you broke it off, but you hadn't written it then. You wrote it just eighteen months ago. You'd signed it and dated it as you always did your poems.'

Camilla caught her breath in, and her hand went to her mouth.

He was smiling. 'You're beginning to catch on. I've no idea how it got into that anthology of verse, but I think Edie must have been guided to borrow it last week. She came upon it. And, as she put it, seeing you were still going round perversely declaring you'd never kept a lamp lit in the window for me, the best thing she could do was to give it to me as proof positive.'

He unfolded it, keeping her within the circle of his arm, and asked, 'How *did* it get in that book?'

She swallowed, but managed to say, 'I wrote it one day last year when for some reason I was absolutely desperate with longing for you and thought I'd never see you again and, as I always do, got it out of my system—as I thought—by writing down quite boldly: "To Jonathan." Once I write my own verses down, it commits them to memory for me, so I was going to burn it. But after I wrote that last verse I had a niggly feeling that I'd read something like it before, so just for my own satisfaction, I looked through every book of poems likely to have that sort of verse in it.

'I didn't think I had the piece of paper with me when I went through the downstairs bookcases. I thought I'd left it in my room. I searched everywhere most frantically, then downstairs, but not in the books.'

Jonathan said, 'It will go into our family treasures. Some day *our* small Peregrine will pass it on to *his* daughter perhaps and tell her that but for that verse she might never have existed.' They read it together slowly, and lingered on that last verse:

'A thousand years from now, a thousand years,
  Time when my body shall be dust and rain,
If I but hear the whisper of your voice,
  I'll stir again.'

He said; and his voice was husky with the ardency of his feelings, 'Do you wonder I love Edie? Love her jangly bracelets, her floating scarves, her clangers . . . she gave me back what I thought had gone for ever. *Now* will you lose your fears?'

Camilla put up her hands, drew his bruised and scratched face down to hers.

Uncle Edward turned the radio off and gave a warning cough. 'We're almost into Whangarei. The traffic's dense, so you could have onlookers. This is my first peek and very interesting I find it. We'll be at the hospital soon.'

They wasted no time afterwards. They wanted to get the evening meal over so they could settle to the regional programme, *Top Half*, at seven-thirty. Jonathan said, 'I hope it's on tonight so we can get it over and done with. The phone will ring all night after it. I must ring Prue and tell her to watch. As soon as this fuss is over you and I can get on with our future. Once you cough up whatever's bugging you, love, we'll set a wedding date, not too far away, either, but we'll have to give my family long enough notice to get their plane bookings. Look, tomorrow we'll pack a lunch and head for Opito Bay and go through that gap in the cliffs—sheer solitude. Camilla, can you imagine what it did to me, so soon after Edie giving me that poem and filling me with hope, when Sylvie said that piece to Greg about him not being on his own for long? But at least you told me what *that* meant.'

She bit her lip. 'I wish the other was as easy. But I'm glad we can't talk it out tonight, darling. I can tell your head is throbbing madly, and I don't want to make it worse.' She hoped that with tomorrow's dawn she would find wisdom and courage.

Everyone connected with the rescue decided it would be more exciting to see it all together and turned up at Hallows House. After all, it was rather fun, with the doctor and the Vicar providing the lighter touches and Jonathan the romance and Gary's parents making everyone realise what it had meant to them to have their son safe and well. What surprised them was that the wedding photographers had provided stills of the elegance of the day before to provide a contrast.

Camilla said, 'Oh, if only the bridal pair could have seen this, but there's no chance, on the island.'

Elinor said proudly, 'They're at Lantana Cove right now, seeing it. I didn't know about the wedding pictures, of course, but I thought they'd want to see this, so I rang Sylvie's father and he got them in his launch.'

They finished at eleven with sandwiches and coffee. Edie was in fine form, of course, and Camilla was apprehensive about that, but apart from looking at the pair of them meaningly now and then she didn't give away to all that she'd been the instrument of reconciliation. They themselves gave no hint that they still had something serious to discuss, but Jonathan said firmly just before the visitors departed, 'Tomorrow Camilla and I are having a day off on our own—a picnic. It's been very entertaining and exciting for the lookers-on, but we owe ourselves some privacy now. Don't expect to see us all day.'

Aunt Rose said promptly, 'Edward and I will come over at nine. It will do you both good. I'll bring your lunch over—no getting up early to cut sandwiches, Camilla.'

Camilla woke early, too early, and lay knowing the day she had dreaded was upon her. She saw the sun rising in splendour on the shining waters guarded by the Gate of Heaven. One ray struck right down on Peterson's Island where Chris and Sylvie were honeymooning, and she envied them that their romance had never known a shadow of mistrust or disharmony. The tranquil beauty of the scene mocked her.

Jonathan had said to her last night, 'Wear that pink skirt and pretty blouse you wore the day we went to the Galbraiths'. You looked delectable enough to eat that day. No shorts, I want you to look all woman.'

She'd liked that. She slipped it on, fastened in some very old-fashioned earrings carved in an enamel-like substance, like tiny roses, touched her wrists and ears with Black Rose perfume, then came down to a breakfast Gran had prepared herself.

Jonathan had on a suit he'd had made in Singapore overnight on his way out, a linen suit, safari style, in buff colour, elegant and cool-looking. It showed off his dark good looks. Suddenly her spirits lifted. Just as Edward and Rose came in, Jonathan kissed Camilla, said, 'Good morning, love, you look just right for this day that life owes us.'

Aunt Rose gave a happy sigh. Uncle Edward, unknown to them, was wondering if he'd ever know how these two had got themselves sorted out after that thumper of a row in the summerhouse.

'Your Day of Destiny,' said Aunt Rose sentimentally. 'What do you mean?' asked Camilla curiously.

Rose looked puzzled. 'Blest if I know. Only here you are, engaged again, and thus far you haven't had a moment to yourselves. Now eat up. I want you out of it before anything crops up urgently in the showroom, or people start getting stuck behind waterfalls or falling off jetties. It looks peaceful enough . . . the schoolchildren have just trooped into school, the bread-van is at the store, Wilma has come early and the Vicar is working in his garden and looking far more respectable than he did on Sunday night, that's for sure . . .' She paused, and they swung round to look at her. She added hollowly, 'But here's Joe Moorie stopping outside our gate. Haven't seen him for years. Well, there's one thing, he can't want either of you, so you'll be able to get away just the same.'

Camilla choked over her toast. *Joe Moorie!* Oh, no, not now. And why? What horrible coincidence had brought him here right now? But she was soon to know it wasn't a coincidence at all.

Jonathan said quietly, 'I rather think it just might be me he wants to see. I think the TV programme has triggered this off. I suppose he didn't know till he saw it that I've returned to New Zealand. Though how he got here at this hour of the morning I don't know. He's still in Whangarei, I suppose? I know his mother lived there and he wasn't far away.'

Camilla felt a wave of nausea rise within her. Jonathan was going to be exposed in front of everyone. Joe would be very angry, even after all these years. He must be, to come here, hot-foot, at this hour. She said hurriedly, 'You'd better see him alone, Jonathan—I mean if it's something private to you.'

But Edward had the door on to the verandah open and Joe was stepping into the room. He said, 'Hullo, everyone,' but it was towards Jonathan he was striding, with outstretched hand. 'Saw the TV programme. I was staying with a friend at Kawakawa. I'd no idea you were in New Zealand or believe me, I'd have been over before. Man, it's good to see you! Letters are so inadequate. You restored my faith in antique dealers. Your generosity and your grandfather's left us without words. The whole collection is now safely in Auckland museum where everyone connected with Tawhiri can see it.'

He turned to the others. Camilla was a little in the background.

'Has Jonathan told you since he came back? At the time I asked him to say nothing because I felt Tawhiri's other descendants would have been hopping mad with Mother.' He paused, then said, 'You all look bewildered. I guess he's been too modest to say. Some scoundrelly fellow turned up at her place one day years ago and bought a historic *mere* from her for a paltry sum. Oh, it wasn't paltry to Mother, but if she'd been in full possession of her faculties she'd never have let it go. Mr Lemaire called in to see her later that day, and she told him all about it. He came straight to me and I tried to trace the fellow, but it was no go. Mr Lemaire was going back to England and offered to try to trace it. I never dreamed he'd succeed, but he did.

'The fellow had paid Mother in notes, so there was no hope of tracing him by a cheque. We'll never know how he got it out of the country. Mother vowed he was English, that was all. He sold it to someone who wouldn't reveal his source, but luckily, knowing Lemaire's reputation, he asked them to put it up. He wouldn't let Jonathan buy it, said it must go to the highest bidder, but the buyer, on hearing the story, parted with it, at a small profit, to the firm. But the overall price *wasn't* small. And all they would let me pay for it was what Mother had received for it. Jonathan must have been too modest to tell you, even now.'

'Well, it didn't matter to them,' said Jonathan.

Camilla made a strangled sound that swung them all

round to gaze at her. Her face was paper-white. 'But it mattered to *me*,' she said. 'Oh, *how* it mattered to me!' Her breath caught in a sob. She controlled herself and went on, 'Joe, your mother told me that *Jonathan* diddled her over the *mere*. She did—truly. I went down to ask her, five years ago. Dilys Cranbourne sent me the clipping of the sale. Joe, *why* would your mother say it was Jonathan?'

Jonathan seemed to be beyond speech. But Joe Moorie wasn't. He said, 'I can tell you why. She was just beginning to lose her grip when she sold it, but that was only being muddled in a general sort of way—occasional lapses of memory. But then she rapidly worsened. Doctor said it was due to pinpoint blood vessels in the brain bursting. She began mixing opposites. She'd say: "My bath is too hot," when she meant it was too cold, and when my wife would add cold, she'd get really mad and think my wife was being stupid. Or she'd say boy instead of girl. She knew at first that Jonathan was going to try to trace it, but with the other dealer being English too, she must have got them mixed up. As simple as that—couldn't tell the goodie from the baddie.' He looked helplessly from one to the other.

Jonathan managed to speak. He looked at Camilla and there might have been no one else in the room at all. 'Is this why you broke our engagement? I think it's beginning to add up. Is this why you didn't want me in the firm? Didn't want anyone capable of doing such a thing associated with Hallows Antiques? Why, love, I can understand that. But one thing I must know. Is that also why you accused me of what you did that night some time ago? Remember?'

Uncle Edward, fascinated, thought when Camilla didn't, in fact *couldn't* reply, that she didn't know what Jonathan meant, and before he could stop himself he said, 'That night in the summerhouse.'

The tension snapped. Jonathan said, 'What? How come you knew that? Did Camilla tell——'

Uncle Edward, properly horrified now, said hastily, 'No, of course she didn't tell me. I was on the roof, absolutely petrified. I'd never heard anything like it. I couldn't think how she could have got a bee in her bonnet like that. But I see it all now. But it doesn't matter, does it, Jonathan, I mean now she's explained?'

Camilla said hotly, 'Uncle Edward, of course it matters! That's why we were going off on our own today. I was going to tell Jonathan the truth. Nothing less would do. But I was going to say it was all in the past, that even if he'd robbed the Bank of England, I still loved him.' She stopped and gave a wail. 'Oh, it sounds so *silly*! And I was so wrong. It's not a very good basis for marriage, is it?'

Jonathan almost shouted. 'No, it doesn't sound silly. It sounds wonderful to me. Even though you thought that, and I know how much the reputation of Hallows Antiques means to you, you were still going to take me on.'

Joe looked appalled. 'I couldn't have come at a worse time.'

Jonathan shook his head. 'Man, it was the best possible moment. Don't you see, all of you? She was going to tell me she knew of my supposed chicanery of five years ago, and when in fear and trembling she'd got it out, I would have had to look smug and injured by telling her she'd got it all wrong. Joe, I'm grateful to you.' He looked at Camilla. 'I'm not mad with you, love, only so thankful this leaves no permanent shadow on our lives.'

He smiled at them all. 'I don't think I can take any more audience, folks.' He put his hand in his pocket, withdrew it with a ring in it, a heavy antique ring, gold, with a ruby set in a frame of tiny diamonds. 'I was going to put this on Camilla's finger before she told me her terrible secret, whatever it was. And to tell her that however many skeletons were in the closet, she was mine. But I'm certainly going to put it on in private.

Out with you, wench, and upstairs.'

In a dream she moved before him. 'Upstairs? But why?'

He laughed. 'With all the hoo-ha nobody has thought to switch off the lamp in the window this morning.'

He looked across at Hallie with love in his eyes. 'You told me once, Hallie, that Camilla still had a lamp in the window for me, and it was true. But it isn't needed any more.'

Hand in hand they went up the worn stairs that had known so many happy feet, the stairs they would climb to their own particular heaven through all the coming years. They went into the old master bedroom that would soon be theirs, where the roadmender lamp stood on the sill. Jonathan turned it out.

Below them reached the shining bay beyond the Inlet, dotted with its gross of islands, each like a jewel upon a blue silk gown.

He slipped the ring on, smilingly, looking into her eyes. It felt wonderful, as if it once more enclosed her love. He tilted up the oval face above the rose-petal blouse, 'No more lamps,' he said, 'because "Home is the sailor, home from sea, and the hunter home from the hill." ' He reached her lips, and thereafter was only silence and ecstasy.

Harlequin® Plus

A WORD ABOUT THE AUTHOR

New Zealander Essie Summers was reared on the joy of words and began writing verses at the age of eight. Curiosity was her trademark, and remains so to this day.

At eighteen she submitted her first poem to an Australian magazine and, Essie says, "It came back home across the Tasman Sea so fast it was hard to believe that the editor had read it!" Her second submission was accepted, however, and she went on to write and have published articles and short stories, as well as poetry.

Her first novel was a romantic mystery, which she submitted to Mills & Boon. On their advice, she cut out all the "skulduggery" and made her story a straight romance. "It's never easy to make such a radical change," she explains, "but my chance was opening before me and I was dazzled by the prospect."

Today, Essie and her husband, Bill, a retired clergyman, make their home in a scenic town on New Zealand's North Island. They are the parents of two children and the grandparents of seven.

Great old favorites...
Harlequin Classic Library

The HARLEQUIN CLASSIC LIBRARY
is offering some of the best in romance fiction—
great old classics from our early publishing lists.

Complete and mail this coupon today!

FREE
BONUS
BOOK

Harlequin Reader Service

In U.S.A. P.O. Box 52040
Phoenix, AZ 85072-2040

In Canada 649 Ontario Street
Stratford, Ontario N5A 6W2

Please send me the following novels from the Harlequin Classic Library. I am
enclosing my cheque or money order for $1.50 for each novel ordered, plus
75¢ to cover postage and handling. If I order all nine titles at one time, I will
receive a FREE book, *Village Doctor*, by Lucy Agnes Hancock.

☐ 136 **Love Is My Reason** (#494)
Mary Burchell

☐ 137 **This Merry Bond** (#583)
Sara Seale

☐ 138 **The Happy Enterprise** (#487)
Eleanor Farnes

☐ 139 **The Primrose Bride** (#988)
Kathryn Blair

☐ 140 **My Heart Has Wings** (#483)
Elizabeth Hoy

☐ 141 **Master of Hearts** (#1047)
Averil Ives

☐ 142 **The Enchanted Trap** (#951)
Kate Starr

☐ 143 **The Garden of Don José** (#928)
Rose Burghley

☐ 144 **Flamingoes on the Lake** (#976)
Isobel Chace

Number of novels checked @ $1.50 each =	$	_____
N.Y. and Ariz. residents add appropriate sales tax	$	_____
Postage and handling	$	.75
	TOTAL $	_____

I enclose _____
(Please send check or money order. We cannot be responsible for cash sent
through the mail.)

Prices subject to change without notice.

Name _____
(Please Print)

Address _____
(Apt. no.)

City _____

State/Prov. _____ Zip/Postal Code _____

Offer expires November 30, 1984   CL-116   40556000000